365 Bedtime Bunny Tales

text: Maike Karstkarel
illustrations: Maan Jansen

Copyright © 1996 by Rebo International b.v., Lisse, The Netherlands

This 2005 edition published by Backpack Books, by arrangement
with Rebo International b.v.

Backpack Books
122 Fifth Avenue
New York, NY 10011

ISBN 0-7607-7272-X

Printed and bound in Slovenia

05 06 07 08 09 MCH 10 9 8 7 6 5 4 3 2 1

Illustrations: Christl Vogl
Cover design: AdAm Studio, Prague, The Czech Republic
Translation: Guy Shipton for First Edition Translations Ltd, Cambridge, Great Britain
Typesetting: Hof&Land Typografie, The Netherlands
Prepress services: AdAm Studio, Prague, The Czech Republic
Proofreading: Emily Sands, Eva Munk and Karen Taschek

365 Bedtime Bunny Tales

text: Maike Karstkarel
illustrations: Maan Jansen

BACKPACKBOOKS

NEW YORK

The wild wood

Somewhere among the hills, right
next to the sea, lies the Wild Wood. In the middle
of that wood lives the Fluffytail family: Father
Fluffytail, Mother Fluffytail and the Fluffytail
children. They all have long ears, little button noses,
strong feet for hopping and, of course...short, fluffy
tails.
Have you already guessed what kind of animals
the Fluffytails are? You have? Come along then,
and we'll take a peek inside their hole.

January 2

The rabbit hole at Rabbit Hill

The Fluffytail family lives in a rabbit hole, or burrow, in Rabbit
Hill. There's a warren of rabbit holes in the hillside where ten
rabbit families live. There are so many holes that in the summer
the hill looks a bit like Swiss cheese. But now it's winter. We'll
have to clear away some of the snow before we can take a look
inside the Fluffytail family's burrow. Look, there's their rabbit
hole! We go through a long tunnel to get to the living room. It's
wonderfully warm and cozy. What nice furniture the rabbits
have! Mother Fluffytail has put a colorful tablecloth on the table.
In the cupboard there are thirteen plates and thirteen cups. That's
because Mr. and Mrs. Fluffytail have eleven children. That's a big
family!

8

January 3 The Great Guidebook

Father Fluffytail is reading out loud from the
Great Guidebook for Rabbits. Everything
rabbits need to know is in that book. Every
chapter ends with the words: "And watch out
for Rusty!" Rusty is the big fox. Foxes love the
taste of tender rabbit. The Fluffytails must
always be on the look out for the fox. Luckily,
Rusty has a bright red fur coat. As soon as the
little rabbits see anything red, they all
disappear down their rabbit hole. But Rusty is
also very clever. He's always coming up with
nasty new tricks.

Pah! I'm not scared!

All at once, Father Fluffytail closes the *Great Guidebook for Rabbits*. He's been reading about what rabbits can do in winter so as not to leave tracks in the snow. He finishes as usual with the words: "And watch out for Rusty!"
Ten of his children tremble with fear at the very thought of the fox. Only Roberta says: "Pah! I'm not scared of Rusty!"
Roberta is a brave little rabbit. She'd really much rather be a boy rabbit. When Mother Fluffytail wants her to put on her dress, Roberta grumbles all day long.
More than anything she likes to wear a pair of jeans and an old sweater. And when Mother isn't listening she says to her brothers and sisters: "Just call me Bob from now on!"

January 5

Daisy

Daisy Fluffytail is terribly vain. She's quite different from her sister Roberta, who would actually much rather be called Bob. Daisy can sit for hours in front of the mirror. First, she puts on a large bow, and then she spends ages brushing her fluffy tail.

All rabbits are very proud of their fluffy tails. That's why they take care of them so well. Mother Fluffytail has taught her children how to do it properly. Each morning, they have to give their tails a good washing and drying. Once their tails are dry, they have to be brushed for at least ten minutes. And Daisy brushes hers every day for at least half an hour.

Brrr! It's so cold!

"Get up, children!" calls Mother Fluffytail as she claps her hands. Her eleven children stretch themselves and then dash out of the hole one after the other. They're going to wash their fluffy tails. Meanwhile, Mother sets the table. She's just about to put the thirteenth plate on the table when Daisy comes rushing in again.
"Mother, Mother, the water has frozen and now I can't wash my fluffy tail!"
Mother Fluffytail smiles. "Don't worry, dearest! Give your tail a good rub in the snow. That'll make it just as clean!"
Daisy carefully rubs her fluffy tail in the snow. Brrr! It's so cold on her behind! I hope that there'll be water again tomorrow, she thinks, shivering.

January 7

Two peas in a pod

Hip looks every inch the same
as his twin sister, Hop,
Try to tell the difference and
you'll see you can't, so stop!

The family gets quite confused
when trying to say the right name.
But Hip and Hop just think it's fun
that they are both the same.

"We're just like two peas in a pod,"
they'll sometimes say and smile.
"When we are grown, perhaps we'll change,
but that can wait awhile."

January 8   **Mistake!**

The Fluffytail family is seated at the table. But before they start eating, Father Fluffytail stands behind each chair to see if all the fluffy tails have been well washed.
"Hmmm, good, good, good," he mumbles contentedly to himself. But when he reaches the chairs of the twins, Hip and Hop, he sees one clean and one dirty tail.
"Ugh! Hop! Out you go and wash your tail again!" he grumbles. But what's happening now? The dirty tail stays on its chair and the clean one rushes outside. Then he hears ten rabbit children giggling. Father has made the same mistake again! But that's how it goes - the twins do look so very much alike!

14

January 9

Ribbons off, cap on

Father Fluffytail has had enough. Hip and Hop look much too much alike. So how is he to tell them apart? He thinks and thinks. At last he has an idea! He calls Hip and Hop and says: "From now on, so that I can tell who Hip is and who Hop is, Hop must wear ribbons on her ears."

Hop doesn't think this is a good idea at all. If she has ribbons on her ears, they won't be real twins anymore. She thinks it's so awful she nearly cries.

Mother Fluffytail sees what the problem is. Luckily, she has already thought of something herself. She goes to the cupboard and takes out two caps, a red one and a blue one. The ribbons can come off if Hip promises to always wear the blue cap and Hop the red one. Yippee! Hip and Hop think their caps are out of this world!

January 10

A quiet spot

It's not always fun having ten brothers and sisters. Especially if you like sleeping. And Charlie Fluffytail loves sleeping. As soon as he has the chance, Charlie looks for a quiet spot where he can have a nap. This morning he hid himself behind the curtain.
"Nobody will find me now. I'll be able to sleep peacefully here," he murmurs. With a heavy sigh, he shuts his eyes and drowses off. He's off on a long journey, all the way to dreamland.

January 11

Tarzan Fluffytail

"Snrrrk, snrrk!" comes a noise from behind the curtain.
That sleepyhead, Charlie Fluffytail, is sleeping there and snoring. He's dreaming about the jungle in Africa. In his dream, he's not called Charlie anymore. Instead, he is Tarzan Fluffytail, king of the jungle. He fights with lions, swims faster than the fastest crocodile, and climbs higher than the most acrobatic monkey. Just as he is about to swing on a vine from one tree to another, something grabs hold of him.
"Help! It's Rusty Fox! He's going to eat me up!" cries Charlie, and he wakes up. But instead he sees his mother standing there.
Mother Fluffytail wanted to dust behind the curtain and there she finds Charlie.

Silly

"Did you dream about the fox?" Tom Fluffytail asks
his little brother Charlie.
"Yes, er, no, er, well yes, I did," stammers Charlie.
Should he tell Tom that he was Tarzan in his dream?
No, Tom would laugh at him. Charlie decides not to
tell everything about his dream. "I dreamed that I was
in the jungle and that something suddenly grabbed me.
I thought it was Rusty the Fox," he explains to Tom.
Tom shakes his head: "There aren't any foxes
in the jungle, silly."
Good, thinks Charlie, in that case, tomorrow I'll dream
that I'm Tarzan again.

January 13

If only it was bedtime!

The Fluffytail children usually play indoors in winter. Outside it's
much too cold. And it's not so easy for them to hide from the fox
in all the white snow. But still, what an enormous crush it is with
all eleven children inside! Charlie finds it all very difficult.
Looking for a quiet spot, he disappears outside. But when he falls
asleep outdoors he dreams only about snow and ice. And that
makes him feel even colder!
Exhausted, he creeps back down the hole again. He sticks his
fingers in his ears and thinks: If only it was bedtime!
Then, at least, it would be nice and quiet....

January 14

A musical rabbit

Billy Fluffytail is a funny rabbit. He's crazy about music. He loves guitars and drums. The louder the music, the more Billy likes it.

He's made himself a drum kit from a few hollow tree trunks. He uses two sticks to beat away at them.

"Yeah, yeah, rock 'n' roll!" he sings as he drums along. He keeps on thinking up new songs, beating his drum set at the same time. And to make it all seem more real, he messes up his hair, just like real rock stars. "Yeah, yeah, rock 'n' roll!"

Bit by bit, Father and Mother Fluffytail get more and more tired of it.

They've had Billy's drumming noise filling their ears all day and it's making them go deaf.

"This has just got to stop for once and for all," grumbles Father Fluffytail. "If this goes on any longer, I'll never be able to get that dreadful racket out of my head."

He gets up out of his chair and walks over to Billy. "Stop that at once, Billy," he says strictly, "and go and play outside for a while. Mother and I want a little peace at home for once."

A "cool" instrument

Billy Fluffytail goes outside in a bad temper. He thinks it's incredibly unfair of his father and mother to take away his drum set. "They're so uncool!" he grumbles as he walks through the snow-covered wood. He's so grumpy that he starts to hit things with his drumsticks as he passes.

Just a moment. What was that? One of his drumsticks just hit an icicle. It goes "plink!" What a great sound! Billy starts to look around at once for more icicles. Look, there's a whole row of them over there. After a little practice, Billy quickly learns to play a nice little tune on the icicles.

"This is fantastic, even better than a drum set!" he thinks.

January 16

Gus

Father and Mother Fluffytail have eleven children.
That makes eleven feathery, fluffy tails, eleven sweet
little button noses and eleven pairs of perky ears.
Eleven pairs of perky ears? Not quite. One pair of
little ears is rather floppy and hangs down. They're
Gus Fluffytail's ears.
Gus has a little kink in his ears. That's why they
always point down to the ground.
Gus can't do anything about it.
And as if that wasn't bad enough, Gus always has a
cold as well. In winter, he's the first to catch the flu
and when the Fluffytail children are playing tag,
Gus is always the one who trips over a fallen branch.
Mother Fluffytail always says: "I worry so much
about my little Gus."

January 17

Gosh, it's cold!

It's been snowing all day in the Wild Wood. Snowflakes keep
falling from the sky and swirling about in the cold air.
The Fluffytail children are bored of sitting indoors. So off they
go into the snow outside. Even so, it's soon too cold for them.
"Brrr!" shivers Daisy. "I'm going back inside."
"Oh, don't do that!" shouts her brother Leaper. "If you just keep
jumping up and down fast enough you'll soon warm up." And he
shows her how to do it then and there.
Leaper goes bounce, bounce, bounce all though the snow.
Watch out, Leaper! There's a hole there! Too late! With a great
flump, Leaper disappears under the snow.
"Gosh, it's cold!" cries out Leaper and runs as fast as he can back
indoors. He runs so fast that he zooms past Daisy on the way.

A heart of gold

"What a mess!" complains Mother Fluffytail. Well, what do you expect after eleven little rabbits have been playing in the snow? Everywhere in the rabbit burrow there are little puddles of melted snow. With a sigh, Mother goes to fetch a mop from the kitchen.
"Wait, Mother, I'll help you," says Freckle. Freckle is her eldest daughter. She's called Freckle because her face is covered in little brown dots. Her brothers and sisters tease her sometimes: "Freckle, go and wash your face."
But Mother Fluffytail comforts her by saying to them: "Freckle has a heart of gold."

January 19   **Flu**

You can be sure that around this time every year, the Fluffytail family will get the flu. As always, of course, it started with Gus. His drooping ears went even floppier than usual. His little nose turned completely red. And he sneezed and sneezed: "Atchoo! Atchoo!" Harry, Roberta, Daisy, Tom, Billy, Leaper and the twins soon caught it too. Father and Mother Fluffytail have their hands full with all these sick little rabbits. Luckily, Freckle helps out. She goes around with the thermometer, fills ten hot-water bottles and reads them stories.
"I'm sure that Freckle is going to be a nurse when she's older," says Mother Fluffytail proudly.

January 20

Where is the thermometer?

What a fuss there is in the Fluffytail family's burrow! The thermometer is missing. And it would happen just when ten feverish little rabbits are lying sick in their beds.
Suddenly, Freckle has a thought. She hops over to her brother Billy's bed. Billy's hair is looking even messier than normal.

Freckle searches through his tufts of hair. Just as she thought! There's the thermometer, stuck in Billy's hair. "As soon as Billy's better again he's going to get a haircut," says Mother Fluffytail.

January 21

Feeling sick

Snuffle, snort and sneeze, cough and choke, and wheeze.
Feeling sick is just no fun.
Wrap up warm until it's done.
Sweat and turn and toss.
Fever makes you cross.
Just blow your nose and say, "I'll stay in bed today."

January 22

How boring

The Fluffytail children are feeling a little better.
They're over the worst of it. Their temperatures have
gone down and they're not coughing so much
anymore. Even so, they still have to stay in bed for
a few more days. "To recover completely," says
Mother Fluffytail.
Harry Fluffytail has had more than enough of staying in bed all the time.
He's so bored by it all.
Harry tosses and turns underneath the bedcovers.
"I've never felt so bored in all my life," he moans to his pillow.

January 23

Are you all asleep yet?

If you've been lying in bed all day long, it's sometimes hard to
get to sleep at night. That's how Harry Fluffytail feels tonight. Even
though it's been dark outside for ages, he still
can't keep his eyes closed.
"I wonder if the others are already sleeping?"
he says to himself. "Hey!" he whispers. "Are
you all asleep yet?"
"No, and if you don't keep quiet we'll never get
to sleep!" mumble his brothers and sisters.
What a bunch of spoilsports, thinks Harry.
Hang on a moment, I'll show them!

January 24

A ghost

Very softly, Harry pulls the sheet off his bed. It's already pitch black in the Fluffytail children's bedroom. Harry creeps past the little beds on tiptoe. Then he pulls the sheet over his head and calls out in a spooky voice: "Wooo! Wooo! I am the ghost of darkness!" His brothers and sisters wake up with a start. Daisy lets out a scream and jumps onto her pillow. And the frightened twins huddle closely together. Then the light comes on. Father Fluffytail has come to see what all the hullabaloo is about. Oh dear. Harry is in trouble now!

January 25

In the loft

"I'm going to show you what we do with ghosts in this house!" growls Father Fluffytail. "You've frightened your brothers and sisters very badly. As punishment you can go and sleep in the loft all night." So that's where poor Harry ends up. All alone in the dark loft. He can hear rustling and creaking noises everywhere. The longer it goes on, the more scared he becomes. The whole night long he doesn't dare shut his eyes for an instant, but the one thing you can say is that it certainly isn't boring! The next day, when his brothers and sisters are allowed to go out and play, Harry is so tired that he creeps straight back to his own comfortable bed.

January 26

Surprise

All the Fluffytail children were
extremely well behaved when
they had the flu. They stayed in
their beds and were very good about
drinking their nasty medicine.
       Even Harry was a perfectly behaved little rabbit, all
things considered. That's the reason why Father and Mother Fluffytail
think they all deserve a reward. From the shop in the woods they have
bought a pair of ice skates for each of their children.
How happy the little Fluffytails are with their surprise! They all
want to try out their new skates immediately, of course.

January 27

Off to the pond

Father and Mother Fluffytail and their eleven children set
off for the pond one behind the other. The water in the pond
has frozen solid and shines like a mirror. It makes a perfect
skating rink for trying out the Fluffytail children's new
skates.
It's a long way for them to go, but at last the little rabbits
can see the ice twinkling in the distance. All at once, they
start hopping a little faster.
"Who's going to be first on the ice?" shouts
Leaper, and off he runs.

January 28

Laces

The Fluffytail children are sitting in a row between the reeds, their cheeks all rosy from the ice-cold air. They tie their laces underneath their skates. But that isn't such an easy thing to do when you're wearing woolly mittens. Leaper is the first one on the ice. The others quickly join him. But what's going on? No sooner have Hip and Hop stepped onto the ice than they are lying flat on their backs! And the others are splitting their sides with laughter. Hip and Hop had been sitting so close to each other that they tied their shoelaces together by mistake. Isn't that just typical of twins!

January 29

Skating takes practice

What a happy sight! All those little rabbits skating on the ice. Leaper, Tom and Roberta quickly get used to it. The others find it a little harder. Father and Mother Fluffytail patiently help their children to skate. All at once, even Gus finds he is able to keep his balance. He proudly skates off on his own. But oh my goodness! His droopy ears are flopping about over his eyes. He can't see where he's going anymore! Crash! With a bump he lands in the reeds. Lucky for him that he's got a good fluffy tail. He doesn't feel anything from his fall. He just gets up and happily skates off again.

January 30

Cold winter evenings

In January, it gets dark very early in the Wild Wood. The wind howls outside and snowflakes swirl all about. In the Fluffytails' burrow it's warm and cozy. A fire crackles in the fireplace and all the Fluffytails sit in front of it. On cold winter evenings like this, Father Fluffytail reads from the *Great Guidebook for Rabbits*. That might sound boring, but this book contains more than just good advice. There are also many exciting stories in it. Most of all, the children like listening to the story of Wild Woodsman Dan. Wild Woodsman Dan was a rabbit hero who was too clever for all the poachers and Rusty the Fox.

The Fluffytail children plan to be just as brave as Wild Woodsman Dan when they grow up. Then they'll also be far stronger and cleverer than Rusty the Fox.

January 31

Wild Woodsman Dan

Who's the rabbit late at night
whom fox or cat does not affright?
Who's too smart for any man?
That is Wild Woodsman Dan.

Who's the one who laughs at dangers?
Outsmarts poachers, hunters, rangers?
None scares villains as he can.
His name's Wild Woodsman Dan.

And who will grow up just as tough
to play on Rusty tricks enough?
Who won't be scared of monsters great?
The Fluffytails! That's who! Just wait!

Rusty the Fox

There are many animals in the Wild Wood who love going to Rabbit Hill. There's always something to see. The father and mother rabbits have so many children. Not a day passes without there being something to laugh about.

But there is just one animal who doesn't come to join in with all the fun. That is Rusty. Rusty is a huge fox with a beautiful red tail and razor-sharp teeth. Rusty the Fox would just love to have a delicious mouthful of tender rabbit to eat every day. That's why he finds it hard to keep away from Rabbit Hill for long. As soon as he sees a little rabbit, he springs off after it. It's a good thing that the rabbits are clever and quick-footed. They have long ears that help them hear even the smallest twig break. And they sniff out any suspicious smells with their little noses. They already know that Rusty is around long before he can jump out of the bushes.

When Rusty the Fox goes to bed on an empty stomach yet again, he says: "Well, I'll be bunny-hopped! Better luck tomorrow!"

February 2

Brave rabbits

When Harry, Leaper and Roberta asked their mother if they could go for a morning stroll, she gave them a thoughtful look at first.
She said: "It is dangerous, you know. The snow has made everything white and you won't be able to hide anywhere. What will you do if Rusty the Fox sees you?"
Leaper says: "In that case, I'll leap out of the way."
Harry says: "In that case, I'll play a trick on him."
And Roberta says: "We're brave rabbits and brave rabbits can deal with Rusty. No problem."

February 3

Tracks in the snow

So off they go. Harry, Leaper and Roberta Fluffytail hop away through the snow. The low sun is shining and they're having the greatest time. Now and then, they throw snowballs at each other. They slide down hillocks on their backs. And sometimes they race one another. They're having so much fun that they don't notice that they're leaving an enormous amount of tracks behind themselves in the snow. The tracks left in the snow by three sets of rabbit feet show everyone exactly where Harry, Leaper and Roberta have gone. Everyone.... and that means Rusty the Fox too.

February 4

Wisdom is better....

The three little rabbits have already
gone a long way when Roberta
suddenly stops and stands still.
"Watch out, everyone! I can smell the fox. It's
not strong yet, but it's coming closer!"
Leaper and Harry stick their noses in the air.
Yes, Roberta is right. What should they do now?
They can't beat Rusty the Fox. He's much too strong for them.
Luckily, Harry has an idea: "Let's go backward the way we came. Then
our tracks in the snow will point in the opposite direction to
where we are. Before Rusty knows what's going on we'll be far away."
"What a good idea!" shout the other two. "Naturally," says Harry, pleased
with himself. "Wisdom is better than strength."

February 5

Birthday

It's Gus Fluffytail's birthday. Mother has brushed his tail as well as she can. Father has hung up paper chains all over the room. And his great big droopy ears do look perkier than usual today. Being the birthday boy is great fun, even for someone like Gus who has so much bad luck. Whenever it's someone's birthday in the Fluffytail family they're allowed to choose what they would like to eat as a treat. Gus didn't have to think for very long about it. He'd known for ages what he wanted: carrot porridge with honey cakes!

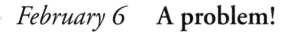

February 6   **A problem!**

Mother Fluffytail takes her husband into the kitchen. She looks a little worried and Father asks what is wrong.
"Gus asked for carrot porridge for his birthday treat. But when I looked in the pantry I couldn't find a single carrot. Now I won't be able to make him any carrot porridge and I feel so sad for little Gus. He's always so unlucky!"
Father nods. "Yes, that is a problem! If our carrots have all been eaten, then there's nothing we can do about it. We won't be able to find any carrots outside in wintertime. What shall we do?"

February 7   Just enough

Freckle was standing just next to the kitchen door. By accident, she overheard what Mother and Father were saying: that there weren't any carrots to make carrot porridge with for her brother Gus's birthday.

How awful! thought Freckle. All the carrots have been eaten! Poor little Gus! Freckle thought long and hard. Perhaps I can find something else that he'd like to eat just as much. She slipped into the pantry and looked on all the shelves and inside all the cupboards. It took her a whole hour, but at last, in a dark corner, she found one big fat carrot that must have rolled off the shelf. Just enough for a little bowl of carrot porridge.

February 8

Birthday treat

Mother Fluffytail sets the table for the birthday party. Afterward, she brings in two pans from the kitchen: a large pan and a little pan. In the large pan, there is ordinary porridge and in the little one, there is carrot porridge! Once all thirteen Fluffytails are seated at the table, they began to sing "Happy Birthday" to Gus. Before Father Fluffytail serves up the porridge into the bowls, he places the little pan in front of Gus. "There! You may have the whole pan all to yourself!" Gus's eyes open wide as he looks at it. A whole pan of carrot porridge just for him! What a wonderful birthday treat!

35

Reading

Tom just sits there all day long,
all curled up in a nook.
Through his glasses peer his eyes.
His nose stuck in a book.

He's reading in the daytime and
at nighttime by moonrise.
He reads, and squints, and reads some more
until he gets crossed eyes.

He reads, and reads, and reads more still.
All books, small or fat.
Except the Rabbits' *Great Guidebook*.
Tom may *not* read that!

February 10

Where's my book?

"Have you seen my book anywhere?" Tom Fluffytail asks his brother Harry. "Your book? No. What are you going to do with a book anyway?" says Harry. "Read it, of course, you dope," says Tom, annoyed. "I want to read and I can't do that without having a book first." Harry wants to help him, but even with the two of them searching they cannot find Tom's book. Tom looks more and more miserable. Suddenly Harry has an idea: "Why don't you read the *Great Guidebook for Rabbits*?" Tom is shocked: "Father doesn't let anyone do that. Only he is allowed to read it." "Aw! Go on, Tom," says Harry. "Father isn't here at the moment, and I won't tell." Oh! Oh!

February 11

Caught!

In fact, children are strictly forbidden to read the *Great Guidebook for Rabbits*. But Tom went ahead and did even so. He secretly took the book and read it while his father was away. Tom quickly put the book back as soon as Father Fluffytail came home. That way Father Fluffytail wouldn't notice anything!

In the evening, Father Fluffytail called to Tom. "Tom, have you been reading the *Great Guidebook*?"

Tom turned from white to red and back again. He started to feel all hot and flustered. How could Father have found out? Then, Father Fluffytail opened the book and there, stuck in between two pages, were Tom's glasses.

Tom had been caught!

February 12

Freckles

Freckle gazes sadly into the mirror. She's looking at her
face.

How ugly freckles are! she thinks. If only my face was pretty
and white, or brown all over. All those spots on my face look
just dreadful.

She sighs deeply. Then she stands up, picks up her mirror and takes
it with her under her arm. She's going to hide it somewhere so that
she never has to look at it again.

February 13

Ugly

"Hey! Freckle, where are you going with that mirror?"
Tom Fluffytail asks his sister with great surprise.
Freckle nearly goes on her way without answering, but then she
stops, takes a deep breath, and explains: "I'm much too ugly
to have a mirror. That's why I'm going to hide it somewhere."
Tom looks at his sister in astonishment. He doesn't think
she's at all ugly and says so too: "What do you mean 'ugly'?"
"I don't want to see all those horrible freckles on my face
anymore," says Freckle. Tom can't understand it. He thinks
that the freckles are what make her look so nice.

February 14   Just like a girl

That's just like a girl, thinks Tom Fluffytail.
His sister Freckle thinks she's ugly because she has
freckles. He decides to cheer her up. "Let's go for a
walk together," he says, "then we can talk about it.
That's sure to help." Together they hop off into the
wood. They talk and talk without paying any
attention. Suddenly, a huge, red beast leaps out in
front of them: it's Rusty the Fox. Oh goodness
gracious, what will they do now?

February 15

A nasty disease

So there they stand. Tom and Freckle Fluffytail
eye to eye with Rusty the Fox.
Rusty licks his lips. Tom has to think as fast as
lightning. All at once he has an idea. "You'd
better watch out, Rusty! We both have a very
nasty disease. The first thing that happens is
that your face gets covered in little spots. Just
take a look at my sister. It's already started
with her!" "Well, I'll be bunny-hopped!" says
Rusty with alarm, and he shuts his eyes
tight. And before he's had time to
open them again, Tom and
Freckle are long gone.
Freckles have their uses
after all!

February 16   The loft

The Fluffytails' rabbit burrow is just
enormous. There are dozens of passage-
ways under the ground that lead to just
as many different rooms.
Mrs. Fluffytail's kitchen is quite close to
the entrance. Otherwise it would be too far
for her to carry all the shopping indoors.
Further inside the burrow are the bedrooms.
One for Father and Mother and one very big one
for all the children. And then there are other rooms,
which are not meant for living in, like the pantry and the
attic. The attic is the highest up of all the rooms in the
rabbits' burrow. Of course it is, I hear you saying to yourself: why,
human beings also live in houses where the attic is right at the top
of the house. Yes, but the Fluffytails' attic is still under the ground
even so. Isn't that a funny thought? An attic underground.

The workshop

Father Fluffytail is really very good at making things. He made all the furniture in the rabbit burrow by himself. He put together all the tables and chairs, the cupboards and even the beds. Making the beds was the most difficult thing he had to do. He sometimes made mistakes while he was making the first, second and third beds. But he made beds number four, five, six, seven, eight and nine in no time at all. But by the time he reached beds number ten, eleven and twelve, he sometimes had to stop and let out a big yawn. Father Rabbit made all those beds in his workshop.

February 18 The carpenter

"Kerbang" went the hammer as it sped down
and hit the old nail upon its head.
"Zishhh" went the saw until late at night,
cutting the planks to a size just right.
A carpenter is Fluffytail, whose skill is plain
to see. From wood he can make anything,
from any kind of tree.
Since he does it just for fun,
he has made for everyone
eleven beds plus one big one
where he'll now rest, his work all done!

February 19

Brrr! it's cold!

"Yippee! I love the winter!" shouts
   Leaper happily.
   "Yes, *you* do," grumbles his little brother
   Charlie, "but then you're also very good at
jumping."
"That's true," cries Leaper and springs high into the air a few
times. He scatters the snow in all directions.
Brrr, Charlie shakes off the snow. Yes, he does think the snow
looks nice but, no, it's much too cold for his feet.
If only I didn't sink up to my ears in the snow all the time, he thinks.
Perhaps it would help if I tied a couple of wooden planks to my feet.

February 20
Slippery planks

The snow has made Charlie Fluffytail's feet much too cold! That's why he has gone looking for two planks of wood and then ties them to his feet. That feels better! "Hey! Leaper, just look at me!" he calls out to his brother. Leaper looks at him with his mouth wide open. What is Charlie up to now? Charlie starts to move forward. But the little wooden planks under his feet are rather slippery. Before he knows what's happening, he starts to slide away. He slides faster and faster down Rabbit Hill. Then, with a great plop, he lands in a heap of snow.

February 21   Skis

I'm never going to tie planks to my feet ever again, thinks Charlie. When you're on the snow you just slide off. He takes off the planks and is about to throw them away when Leaper says to him: "Don't do that! Can I have your planks? They're the best skis that I've ever seen." "Of course you can," replies Charlie. "So long as I don't have to do any skiing with you. One crash in the snow is quite enough for me." "Scaredy-cat!" teases Leaper, and off he goes on the skis. He has the most splendid fun all afternoon while Charlie sits nice and snug next to the stove.

February 22

What a waste

Mrs. Fluffytail shakes her head. She looks inside the bucket that she has just taken out of the pantry. There are potatoes in it. Some of them still look good. But here and there, there are a few old wrinkly ones.
"What a waste!" sighs Mrs. Fluffytail. "I'll have to throw away half of these potatoes. They can't be eaten anymore. It's lucky that we still have enough to last the winter."
"Don't throw them away, my dear!" says Father Fluffytail. "Even potatoes that are too old to eat can be useful."

February 23

Shapes and patterns

Mother Fluffytail and her eleven children look at Father in amazement. What could Father want with potatoes that are too old too eat?
Father chuckles to himself. He takes out his penknife and cuts one of the potatoes in half. On the flat side, he cuts out a little shape. "Children, just go and fetch your paint box and a sheet of paper."
Still gazing at him in wonder, they go and do as he says. Then, Father colors in the little shape with bright red paint and presses the potato onto the paper. When he takes the potato away they all see a cheery little red rabbit shape left on the paper.

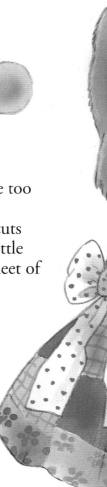

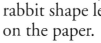

Potato printing

All eleven Fluffytail children watch their father with mouths wide open. Using the old potatoes, he cuts out one pattern after another, all of them different. He makes triangles, circles, squares, rabbit shapes and lots more besides. Next, he says to his children: "Now go and make a pretty picture with the paint and potato shapes."
The Fluffytail children set to work at once. At first it's quite difficult, but they soon get better at it. By printing a long stripe shape with a triangle on top they can make a fir tree. By printing a square shape with a triangle above it they can make a house. They're happy all afternoon and make the prettiest patterns.
Father Fluffytail winks at his wife, and she thinks how clever he is.

February 25   **What is Daisy doing?**

"Has Daisy gone out again?" asks Mrs. Fluffytail, surprised. "Usually she's indoors as soon as the first snowflake starts to fall. And now that it's freezing she's out all day." The other Fluffytail children can't understand it either. So they decide to go off and find Daisy. "If Roberta, Harry and Leaper go along the edge of the wood, and Hip, Hop and Gus go to the heath, then Charlie and I can go and look around Rabbit Hill," says Tom. "And what about me?" asks Billy. "Oh you wouldn't be able to see anything anyway with all that hair in front of your eyes," the others tease him. They're so unfair, thinks Billy, and he hops off in a temper.

Stupid mirror

Billy Fluffytail grumbles to himself crossly as he hops away. His brothers and sisters always tease him about his long hair. They say: "Hey, Billy, did you lose your comb?" or, "Is that your front or your back?" or "Silly Billy Bird's-Nest Hair!"
"Do I really look so silly?" he wonders out loud. By now he has reached the pond. Its water is frozen solid and shines in the sun like a mirror. Billy bends over to take a look at himself in the ice and sees his tangled mess of hair. It's sticking up all over the place in little spikes. It looks just terrible! "Stupid ice mirror!" growls Billy and he feels like stamping on the ice until it breaks.

February 27   ## A vain little creature

Billy Fluffytail is just about to break up all the ice on the pond. "Leave my mirror alone!" Daisy shrieks to her brother. Billy is scared out of his wits. He hadn't noticed that Daisy was standing next to the pond as well. He suddenly understands why Daisy has been going outdoors so much in the last few days. Daisy is such a vain little creature that her little mirror at home isn't enough for her. So long as the pond stays frozen, she can have the biggest mirror in the whole of the Wild Wood to look at. Oh well, thinks Billy, if Daisy really likes looking at herself so much, he'll leave her mirror alone.

February 28

Crying trees

All at once, the freezing weather
is over. The snow on the trees is
melting. Great drops of water drip from
the branches to the ground. Plop! Plop!
Great fat tears are falling from Charlie Fluffytail's eyes.
"What is the matter, Charlie?" asks Freckle.
Charlie sniffs and says: "I feel so sad."
"But why is that?" Freckle wants to know.
"It looks just as if the Wild Wood is crying," replies
Charlie. "Just look around. Even the trees are crying."
Freckle can't stop herself from laughing: "Silly Charlie,
why, the trees aren't crying at all.
In fact, I think they're glad that all the cold
weather is over."

February 29

Tears

It isn't always true, you know,
that tears are signs of spirits low.
Quite often you will laugh so much
that you can't speak. You feel so
touched
a tear will roll down from your eyes,
which you can leave until it dries.
All tears like that tell me you're glad;
that you're a happy lass or lad.
And if you're laughing, child of mine,
then you must certainly feel fine.

49

March 1

True stories

"Wow!" gasps Charlie Fluffytail when Father shuts *The Great Guidebook for Rabbits*. Father has just read them a story about Wild Woodsman Dan. There are many stories in the *Great Guidebook* about the fearless rabbit hero, Wild Woodsman Dan. Wild Woodsman Dan lived long, long ago in the Wild Wood. At that time, the wood was full of many dangers, even more than it is today. But Wild Woodsman Dan was scared of nothing and nobody. When Father Fluffytail reads out one of Wild Woodsman Dan's stories, all the little Fluffytails are as quiet as mice. And even Charlie, who's always fidgeting, listens with all ears.
Wild Woodsman Dan had the most exciting adventures and they're all true stories!

March 2

Hero

Wild Woodsman Dan is the Fluffytail children's hero. He was a brave rabbit who lived a long time ago in the Wild Wood. At that time, it was a huge, dark forest full of dangers. But Wild Woodsman Dan was not afraid. He was a clever, jolly rabbit full of courage. He wasn't even scared of the fox.
He tramped through the forest all day long, armed with his catapult and his bow and arrow. He carried a bag on his back in which he kept all kinds of things: string, a penknife, berries and lots more besides.
Anything, in fact, that might come in handy.

March 3

Just like Wild Woodsman Dan

Harry Fluffytail is trying to creep very quietly out of the rabbit burrow. He's taking something with him under his arm. "What have you got there?" asks Mother Fluffytail. Harry is taken by surprise, turns beet red, and stammers: "Oh, nothing. Just a bag." Mother takes a good look. But isn't that her shopping bag that Harry is hiding under his arm? "Just a moment, young rabbit!" she says. "Give that shopping bag back right this minute!" Muttering under his breath, Harry does what his mother tells him. "Now I still don't have a bag to put things in like Wild Woodsman Dan!" he grumbles. "How am I supposed to be a brave rabbit if I don't even have a bag?"

March 4 **Doing the dishes**

"Roberta, it's your turn to do the dishes!" calls her mother. Roberta looks cross and drags her feet as she goes to the kitchen. She doesn't feel at all like doing the dishes! Humph! What a boring job!
Roberta dawdles the whole time. After a quarter of an hour, when Mother Rabbit comes in to see how things are going, Roberta has only done five plates and there are still eight more to be cleaned! She won't be finished for a while yet, thinks Mother Fluffytail.

March 5   Housework

Freckle Fluffytail comes into the kitchen. What's all this? Her sister, Roberta, is still doing the dishes. Well, to be honest, all she's doing is stirring the soapsuds about a bit with the brush. "I hate doing the dishes so much," sighs Roberta. Freckle nods. "No, doing the dishes isn't much fun. But when you grow up and get married you'll have to do the dishes then too." Roberta turns around crossly. "I'm not going to get married, and *if* I do, then my husband can do the dishes as well. As if girls are only good enough for doing housework! When I'm grown up I'm going to do lots of brave things like Wild Woodsman Dan."

March 6   A girl

Cook and scrub and dust and bake.
Feeding babies, beds to make.
"No!" Roberta said. "Not me!
That's as dull as dull can be."
Race and jump and run and fight.
Roaming forests dark as night.
"Yes!" Roberta said. "That's me!
Just like Woodsman Dan I'll be.
Rough and tough and brave," she said.
Can't I be a boy instead?"

March 7

Traps and snares

Very few human beings ever go into the Wild Wood. All the big towns are far away. There are a few farms on the edge of the wood, it's true, but the farmers there are much too busy to take walks in the woods. Even so, the rabbits in the Wild Wood still have to be very careful. Sometimes, as night begins to fall, poachers will come into the wood. They put down hidden traps and snares to catch the forest animals. If a rabbit should fall into one of these snares, then all hope is lost for the poor little thing. Isn't that sad?

March 8 The smell of humans

Tom Fluffytail is hopping through the wood. The sun is shining on his fur. It's a beautiful day. Just right for a good forest run. But Tom still made sure to polish his glasses well before setting off today. The night before, there were men in the woods. They were wearing great big boots and were carrying guns over their shoulders. Father Fluffytail warned his children about them. Those men were called poachers. The Wild Wood would now be full of dangerous traps and snares. "Keep your noses to the wind!" said Father Fluffytail. "If there's a smell of human beings, you can be sure that there's a trap somewhere close by!"

March 9 Trapped

In the middle of the Wild Wood, all the trees and bushes grow very thickly together. Tom Fluffytail is passing through when he hears a frightened whimpering sound nearby. Tom carefully creeps closer. He's scared out of his wits by what he sees. Among the bushes, there hangs a wire snare, and in that snare a rabbit is trapped. It's his little cousin, Rose. Luckily for her, she isn't trapped in the snare by her neck. Only one of her back feet is caught, but that's quite bad enough. Rose looks at her cousin Tom helplessly.
"Poor little Rose," says Tom. "What *can* I do?"

March 10 A kiss

"Boohoo!" sobs Rose. The poor little rabbit has been caught in a snare by her back foot. What a bit of luck it was that Tom Fluffytail just happened to come along and find her. Now that he's there, Rose doesn't feel so alone anymore. But Tom wants to free Rose. He thinks and thinks.... The snare is made of metal wire. That makes it much too tough to bite through. But the poachers have tied the snare to a twig on a bush.
"That's it!" cries out Tom.
"A twig is something I *can* bite through. Then the snare will come loose from the bush. Afterward, we'll just have to see how to get it off your foot when we're home!"
No sooner is it said than the job is done. Tom bites through the twig and off the rabbits hop with snare and all. Back home, all the rabbits lend a hand in taking off the snare and Rose is soon free again. To say thank you, she gives Tom a big kiss and says: "You're just as clever as Wild Woodsman Dan!"

March 11 Nightmares

Old Rusty Fox has awful dreams
of little baby foxes' screams;
of dreadful things that him await;
and that he'll meet a frightful fate.
What kind of terror is it makes
a great big fox so get the shakes?
He's dreaming all night long
about Wild Woodsman Dan
who wants his snout!

March 12 Bags under
the eyes

Rusty the Fox is walking through the wood.
He spent the whole night dreaming. They were the
worst kind of dreams that a fox can possibly have...all
about Wild Woodsman Dan. Of all the rabbits in the wood,
he was the only one who all foxes feared. He was so big,
strong and clever that even the slyest fox could not beat
him. Brrr, shivers Rusty as he thinks about his dreams. And
the fur on his back stands up on end.

56

March 13   Help!

I'll just go and have a little drink of water, thinks Rusty the Fox. He slept so badly the night before that he can't see straight any longer. Perhaps some clean, fresh water will help. The fox walks to the pond and starts lapping up some water with his tongue. Suddenly, he hears a rustling noise behind him. He turns around...and is frightened out of his fur. Out of the bushes comes a giant rabbit! It's at least twice as big as an ordinary rabbit. "Help!" cries Rusty. "Wild Woodsman Dan!" And he dashes off like greased lightning.

March 14   In disguise

Hip and Hop Fluffytail split their sides laughing. They had thought of a fun game to play. First, Hop stood on Hip's shoulders. Next, they wrapped a big blanket around themselves, and with an old hat that they borrowed from a scarecrow, their disguise was complete. Then, they decided to go and look at themselves in the pond. But Rusty the Fox was there. He was completely terrified. "He thought that we were Wild Woodsman Dan for sure," laughs Hop.

March 15

A dirty ruffian

"I don't understand what it is about Woodsman Dan you all like so much," says Daisy to her brothers and sisters with her nose in the air. "All he ever did was fight all the time and I'll bet he never washed himself."
"He was the bravest rabbit in the world!" protest the others.
"I'd like to be as strong and smart as he was," says Harry.
"And I'd like to be as good at making things," says Gus.
"Woodsman Dan is someone even *I* would marry," sighs Roberta.
"A dirty ruffian like that?" scoffs Daisy.
"Better you than me."

March 16

In love

When she's talking to the others, Daisy Fluffytail says that she thinks Wild Woodsman Dan is just a dirty ruffian. But when she's lying in her bed at night she often dreams of him. Sometimes she dreams she is lying trapped in a snare, or else being attacked by Rusty the Fox, or carried off by wicked poachers. But every time, who comes to her rescue? Wild Woodsman Dan, of course! I think that Daisy is secretly a little bit in love with Wild Woodsman Dan.

March 17

A bold knight

A knight who's bold and like a lion,
very tall and strong as iron.
That's how Daisy's hero seems
when Woodsman Dan is in her dreams.

He's so handsome and so clever,
always joking, fearful never.
So Daisy hopes it will come true
That Woodsman Dan will love her too.

But it's a secret in the day.
And that's why she'll say right away:
"That Woodsman Dan is far from nice.
I wouldn't look his way, not twice!"

March 18

The crow hunters

Father Fluffytail opens the *Great Guidebook*. Today, he's going to read one of the stories about Wild Woodsman Dan. It's called "The Crow Hunters" and it goes like this: Long ago, there was a time when the animals of the Wild Wood were bothered by the crow hunters. Now, the crow hunters were rats who flew on the backs of crows as black as soot. They would fly all through the forest and steal all the other animals' food. And so the animals gathered and decided to call Wild Woodsman Dan to help them. Woodsman Dan thought long and hard.

His bow and arrow were of useless because the crow hunters could fly high up into the sky. "I need to fly as well," said Woodsman Dan. He went to his friend the owl for advice. The owl said he would help him. Woodsman Dan climbed onto the owl's back and went after the crow hunters, chasing them out of the forest. Hooray for Wild Woodsman Dan!

March 19   **Are you crazy?**

Leaper Fluffytail lets out a deep sigh. He enjoyed the story about the crow hunters. Wild Woodsman Dan dared to do everything, didn't he? Just like that, on an owl's back, flying this way and that through the air and on top of that shooting arrows at the crow hunters!
"Could I do that too?" he asks his brother Harry.
"What? Flying through the air on the back of a bird with your hands free?" says Harry, shocked.
"Are you crazy? It's much too dangerous!"
But the idea just won't go from Leaper's head.
Oh dear, oh dear. Some trouble or other is going to come of all this!

March 20

Flying

"I have to fly and so I shall," decides Leaper Fluffytail. He asks the wood pigeons if he may fly on their backs. The pigeons just look at him and shake their heads. Next, Leaper goes to the starlings. But they don't think it's a good idea either. And neither do the ducks, nor the blackbirds, nor the woodpeckers.
"I'd like to help you," offers a kind sparrow. But when Leaper tries to sit on the sparrow's back, the little bird disappears completely from sight. No, I think that Leaper is better off forgetting all about flying for the moment.

March 21 **Off to get a haircut**

"Come on, kids!" calls Father Fluffytail, and he claps his hands.
"We're all going off to get a haircut."
The Fluffytail children all go and stand in a row. Father counts their
fluffy tails: one, two, three, four, five, six, seven, eight, nine, ten....
But where is number eleven? Which one of the little Fluffytails is
missing? Harry, Tom, and Gus are there. And Leaper, Charlie, and
Hip and Hop the twins are too. Freckle's there and Roberta.
And let's not forget Daisy, who loves having her hair done.
Do *you* know who it is who is still missing?
"Where's Billy?" booms Father. Nobody knows where Billy is.
Could it be that Billy doesn't *want* to go and get his hair cut?

March 22

Hiding

Billy Fluffytail hates hairdressers. The comb always gets stuck when the hairdresser tries to comb the tangles out of Billy's wild hair. One day a whole hair brush got lost inside it all! That is why the hairdresser always cuts Billy's hair very short. When he gets the chance to do so, that is! For Billy always has an excuse to get out of having his hair cut. Sometimes he says that he has a tummy ache or a headache and sometimes, like today, he just hides himself somewhere. That's how much he hates having his hair cut!

March 23   **Very determined!**

That evening, the Fluffytail children are seated around the dinner table. They've all had their hair nicely cut. Tom even has a little forelock and Daisy two smart braids. Only Billy's hair is messily sticking out all over the place. But then Billy didn't go along with them to the hairdressers. He hid the whole day. "Billy," sighs Mother Fluffytail, "what am I to do with you?" "Leave my hair in peace!" says Billy. "Wild Woodsman Dan never went to the hairdresser either and I'll bet *his* mother didn't moan about it!"

March 24

A ball game

Spring has really arrived! The warm sun is shining through the fluffy white clouds. The Fluffytail children are playing in front of their rabbit hole on Rabbit Hill. Ten of them are standing in a circle and the eleventh is standing in the middle. That is Harry. Harry is holding a lovely red ball. The others have to hold their paws behind their backs. When Harry throws the ball to one of them, they have to try and catch it.
But sometimes Harry only pretends to throw the ball to someone. Then they have to keep their paws behind their backs. What a difficult game it is to play!

March 25

Bad luck

Gus Fluffytail is also playing the ball game.
He's standing in the circle with his arms folded behind his back. His brother Harry throws the ball to him.
But those floppy ears of Gus's are hanging in front of his eyes. He doesn't even see the ball coming. Bonk!
The ball hits him right on the nose.
"Stupid Gus!" shout the others. "You're 'it'!
Now *you* have to stand in the middle of the circle." With a heavy heart, Gus
does what they say.
I always have bad luck,
he thinks.

Even Wild Woodsman Dan...

'Come on, Gus," says Father Fluffytail. "Try and clean your plate for once."
Gus sighs and takes another mouthful.
"Is something wrong?" asks Mother.
There comes another deep sigh. "Why am I so clumsy? I always lose at
games and...and..."
"But darling," Mother smiles, "it only seems that way. You're very
good at other things. Like drawing, for example. You're very
good at that."
"That's true." Gus nods.
"And what's more," adds Father, "all of us are clumsy
sometimes. Even Wild Woodsman Dan was
clumsy now and then."
"Even Wild Woodsman Dan?"
asks Gus in disbelief.
"Yes, even Wild Woodsman Dan,"
reply Father and Mother firmly.

Little Wild Woodsman Dan

The Fluffytail children have thought of a new game to play. It's called Little Wild Woodsman Dan. Nine of them play the part of the rabbits. One rabbit pretends to be Rusty the Fox. And the eleventh Fluffytail rabbit plays the part of Wild Woodsman Dan. The fox tries to catch as many of the rabbits as possible. He does that by touching them. The rabbits who are touched have to go and stand in what they call the fox hole, and the fox keeps a good eye on them all the time. Wild Woodsman Dan has to touch the rabbits in the fox hole to set them free again. Charlie Fluffytail, of course, is the first rabbit to be caught by the fox. As usual, he's just standing there dreaming. "I don't mind," Charlie says to himself. "I can have a nice little nap in the fox hole."

Just as well

Charlie Fluffytail shuts his eyes. Let the others play their tiring games, he thinks. I'll just take a nice quiet nap. It isn't long before he's snoring. He doesn't notice at all that the others have become bored with their game.
"Hey, everyone! Come and see Charlie snoring!" says Harry.
"Shall we play a trick on him?" suggests Leaper.
"What do you want to do?" asks Roberta. "Let's scare him to bits," says Leaper. They start to gather long blades of grass and then bunch them together. It looks very bushy, just like a fox's tail. Then they brush it against sleeping Charlie's nose.
"Help!" cries Charlie, waking with a start. "It's Rusty! It's Rusty!"
Then he sees all the laughing rabbits standing around him. At first, he's angry, but then he feels rather relieved: it's just as well that it wasn't the real fox.

March 29 **Storm**

The howling wind is blowing all around Rabbit Hill.
In the morning, the weather was beautiful, but now it's
raining and blowing a gale.
"I thought it was spring," grumbles Harry Fluffytail.
Harry hates sitting indoors. He's bored to tears.
All at once, he decides he can't stand it any longer.
He puts on his rubber boots and raincoat and leaves
the rabbit burrow.
"Woooo! Woooo!" howls the wind. A strong gust of
wind picks Harry up and carries him off into the air.
Oh gosh! In stormy weather, little rabbits
are better off staying indoors.

March 30 **In the tree**

"Where's Harry?" asks Father Fluffytail.
"Harry went outside."
"What? Outside? In the middle of a storm?
That's far too dangerous!"
Father Fluffytail runs outside at once. He
searches and he searches, but he cannot find
Harry anywhere. Suddenly, he hears a
frightened little voice from somewhere
above him: "Here I am, Father!"
Father Fluffytail looks up and sees
his son stuck in between two tree
branches. The wind had blown
him into a tree. With great
difficulty, Father Fluffytail
manages to get his soaking
wet son down to the
ground. Very relieved,
Harry promises never
to go out in a storm
again.

High, but not dry

Silly little Harry, Father told you, oh so clear:
"Playing games out in a storm is not a good
idea."
But still the silly, fluff-tailed child
just hopped on out into the wild.
The wind thought, "Gosh! Oh, this is great,
At last I have a new playmate."
It picked him up without a thought:
"Aha!" it said. "Look what I've caught!"
It set him down just like a feather,
high in a tree in frightful weather.
It's just as well that Father found
his son, who said when on the
ground:
"Although I had a super view
when I was up so high,
it isn't any fun at all and
certainly not dry!"

April 1 **April fool**

Harry Fluffytail always looks forward to April first. The rest of the year he is punished if he plays jokes on the other children. But on April first it's allowed!
"This year I'll have to think of something really special," he mutters to himself. "Otherwise they'll know at once that I'm teasing them."
He thinks, scratches behind his ear with his foot, and thinks some more.
"Hey, Harry!" he hears his sister Freckle suddenly call. "Have you seen that awful tear in the seat of your shorts? You really can't go around like that, you know!"
Harry is so embarrassed. What? Is there a hole in his shorts? He turns his head almost all the way around to try to see where it is. Then he realizes that Freckle has started laughing until she can't stop. "April fool! April fool!" she calls.
Oh no! What a mean trick! thinks Harry. He has forgotten completely that he was about to play a trick on someone himself.

April 2 **Spring sunshine**

"Ah! It's spring!" sighs Father Fluffytail contentedly. He's sitting pleasantly in the sunshine. "Yes," says Mother Fluffytail, "time for the big spring clean!" "Oh no!" says Father. "Just enjoy the nice weather. You can clean anytime."
Mrs. Fluffytail isn't sure. It certainly is lovely in the sun. But the beds do have to be aired. "Oh really!" says her husband. "Just come and sit next to me." "All right," says Mother, "but in that case I'm calling the children too. The spring sunshine will make their tails grow."

70

April 3 All in a row

There they all are, the Fluffytail family sitting in a row with their fluffy tails in the sun. Mother has told them that their tails will grow in the sun's warmth. "Can you feel your tail growing yet?" Hip asks Hop. "No, I just feel really hot," replies Hop. They are well behaved and keep sitting there for a quarter of an hour. But then they get restless. "Can we go and play now?" whines Leaper. "Oh, go on then," says Father Fluffytail. And scarcely before the words are out of his mouth, all the little Fluffytails have raced off.

April 4 Leaper

Leaper can't sit still for two minutes. At the dinner table, he's always the first to finish eating and then he starts to fidget in his chair. It drives Father and Mother Fluffytail crazy.
"Leaper, just sit still for once!" says Mother.
"Leaper, will you stop fidgeting!" says Father.
And then Leaper really tries his hardest to sit still. But before you know it, he's rocking back and forth on his chair again.
"There's only one thing to do," says Father Fluffytail one day. "We'll have to tie him to the chair." Oh! Oh! That really makes Leaper think twice.

April 5   Fidgeting

If your name is Leaper Rabbit,
you fidget all the day.
You can't stop your wriggling habit.
Never mind what others say.
It drives Leaper's parents crazy.
They say: "Leaper, just sit still!"
But it isn't that he's lazy.
It's his body's own strange will.

April 6   Naughty feet

Leaper
has been punished.
He jumped off his chair at
least ten times at dinnertime,

and he hadn't even finished his supper!
Enough was enough. "Go to your bed,
Leaper!" said Father Fluffytail crossly.
"You can only come back when you've settled
down." But long after they have finished
clearing the table, Leaper has still not come back
downstairs. Father goes upstairs to see what the
matter is with Leaper. He goes into the bedroom
and finds Leaper in bed. He's in floods of tears.
"Now, now, little fellow," says Father gently. "You
mustn't cry, just try not to be so wild at the table."
"But," sniffs Leaper, "I can't do anything to stop
it. I want to sit quietly,
but my feet don't want to."

April 7

The ball

Roberta Fluffytail is over the moon. In her paws she's holding a new ball that's all the colors of the rainbow. The ball is so lovely! And it's all hers!
She has swapped toys with her cousin Rose. Rose now has Roberta's doll with the little white apron, and Roberta has Rose's ball. "I'm so happy with my ball!" sings Roberta. "At last, I can play soccer whenever I want!" And Rose? Rose is thrilled to bits with the doll. She would much rather play with dolls than with a ball. So they're both very pleased.

April 8

Playing alone is boring

Puffing and panting, Roberta Fluffytail runs after her new ball. It's making her feel so hot!
Playing soccer all by yourself isn't really as much fun as she thought it would be. So she goes off looking for someone to play with her. Look, Harry and Leaper are just over there. They want to play. But Harry and Leaper have other plans. They're going fishing. How boring! thinks Roberta. Then she sees her brother Gus. Gus is awfully clumsy but he wants to play soccer. "Well, all right," says Roberta. "Playing alone is boring!"

April 9   **Taking aim**

"Just go and stand over there, Gus!" says Roberta. "Then I'll pass the ball to you." She gently kicks the beautiful, shiny ball. She has aimed well and the ball rolls in a straight line to Gus's feet. "Now you have to kick it back to me!" she explains. Gus knows very well how to play soccer. He can kick very hard. He takes a run up and kicks the ball as hard as he can. But Gus has not aimed so well. Up goes the ball into the air and it disappears among some tree branches. The ball has gone! "You're so clumsy! Look what you've done!" shouts Roberta. "Now I've lost my ball." Together, they search under trees and in bushes, but they cannot find the ball anywhere. With a long face, Roberta sits down under a birch tree. All at once, the wind starts to blow through its branches. And just at that moment, her shiny new ball drops onto her head from up above. The ball wasn't lost after all. It was just stuck between some branches. Thank goodness!

April 10   The conductor

Billy Fluffytail hears music everywhere. If it rains, or
hail falls from the sky, or if the birds are singing in the
wood, he beats out the rhythm with his foot. "Say,
Billy," says a robin one day, "would you like to be the
conductor for our bird choir?" "What's a conductor?"
asks Billy. "A conductor is in charge of the choir singers.
He has a stick that he beats in time to the music.
That's how he makes sure that all the birds in the choir
sing at the right time." "Isn't that terribly difficult?"
wonders Billy. "It's not easy," says the robin, "but you
can do it if you practice hard. I'm sure you can."
Billy starts practicing at once. He wants to do his
very best as the bird choir's conductor.

April 11

Choir
practice

Today, Billy Fluffytail is going off to
practice with the bird choir for the very
first time. The old conductor, Professor
Partridge, helps Billy. He shows him how to
hold the conducting stick. "Look, like this,"
says Professor Partridge and Billy watches.
But Billy has a much better idea: "I can just
stamp the rhythm with my right back foot.
Then the bird choir will not only be able to
see the rhythm of the music, but hear it
too." He starts to stamp straight away.
But all his stamping makes it almost
impossible to hear the sweet
birdsong any more. Not such a
good idea after all, Billy!

76

A good old stamp

A one, a two, a three and a four!
Yes, I can stamp like this ever more.
Oh, see my right foot stamp and stomp,
and see the ground shake as I romp.
A two, a three, a four and a five!
My other foot has now come alive.
Alas, the birdsong is quite drowned.
I'd need ten choirs to hear
their sound.

April 13   Miserable

The others are always playing such rough games! thinks Charlie Fluffytail. I don't like all that hustle and bustle at all. But that's how it is when you have ten brothers and sisters. There's always going to be one who's rowdy and making a racket. That's why Charlie goes looking for a quiet friend; someone who doesn't mind if he's sleepy or daydreaming. "There must be a friend like that somewhere, right?" Charlie says softly to himself, and he sets off.
On the way, he meets with all kinds of animals. But all of them are very hard at work or much too boisterous. The squirrels leap from one branch to another. The field mice do nothing but look for food. And the blackbirds and thrushes are always arguing. It all makes Charlie feel very tired *and* miserable.

April 14   Leaving the wood

Charlie Fluffytail is looking for a friend who is quiet. He goes so far that he reaches the edge of the wood. Alarmed, he looks around.
Oh my goodness! He had no idea that he'd gone so far. What should he do? Should he go back? But he still hasn't found himself a quiet friend. No, decides Charlie, I'll go on until I've found my quiet friend. He hops bravely on. The edge of the wood is bordered by farmers' fields. That is a dangerous place for a small rabbit. But Charlie can only think about finding a new, quiet friend.

A giant!

"How tired you get from all that hopping!" sighs Charlie Fluffytail. He's been off searching for a new friend for hours by now. "I think I'll just have a short rest." He sees a good spot underneath a big wooden fence. But to get there he must cross a sandy path first. Charlie looks to the left and to the right. He can't see anything. Then he quickly runs across the path. Behind the fence long, tall blades of grass are growing. Charlie makes a safe, cozy nest for himself among them. "Phew," he sighs, "it's not easy finding a friend." He closes his eyes and falls asleep. After a while, he wakes up again. Something is tickling his ears. What is it? "Help!" squeals Charlie. "A giant!"

April 16   Barney the horse

Barney the horse was grazing quietly in his meadow. Suddenly, he noticed something lying in the grass. Curious, Barney went over to see what it was. Charlie Fluffytail was lying there asleep. Charlie was woken up by Barney sniffing him. At first, Charlie was terrified. He'd never seen a horse before. My goodness, that horse was so big! But when Barney asked Charlie politely who he was, some of Charlie's old courage returned. "I'm Charlie Fluffytail," he said. "Would you like to be my friend?" "Very much," said Barney. "So long as I don't have to do too much, because I'm happiest just being here in the sun, chewing the grass." "That's just what I like doing too!" cries Charlie happily. He's found himself a quiet, peaceful friend at last.

April 17   Full pockets

Mrs. Fluffytail is going to wash jeans today. Eleven little rabbits mean eleven little pairs of jeans. A whole washing machine full. Before she puts them in, she first empties all the pockets. In Daisy's pockets she finds a little mirror and a bow for her hair. In Leaper and Harry's jeans there are rubber bands and bits of paper. Mother leaves Tom's jeans until last. Do you know why? Tom fills his pockets with anything and everything. Every time he goes on an expedition to the woods he finds a hundred and one things: twigs, leaves, beetles – you just can't begin to imagine. He says he wants to keep all those things. Mother Fluffytail has other ideas. She holds Tom's jeans upside down over the wastebasket. That's better! All neat and tidy!

April 18   Where are my glasses?

Tom Fluffytail has lost his glasses. They aren't on his bedside table and they're not in the living room either.
"Think good and hard, Tom," says Father Fluffytail, "when did you last see your glasses?"
Tom wrinkles his brow and thinks very deeply. "I still had them yesterday because I was reading for a while in bed," he says. "And this morning, we played tag outside after breakfast. Then I put my glasses in my pocket."
"Well, then, they are still there," explains Father, satisfied, and he goes back to reading his newspaper in quiet.
But Tom doesn't feel at all satisfied. The jeans he was wearing that morning were the ones that Mother put in the washing machine!

April 19   To the rescue

Tom Fluffytail runs like lightning to the washing machine. He wants to take his glasses out of his jeans pocket before it goes into the machine. But oh dear! The jeans are already in the machine and the machine is working.
"What should I do now?" wails Tom. "My glasses are sure to be broken inside the washing machine. I'll just have to take them out." He switches the machine off and opens the door. Oh Tom, you are silly, just look! As soon as the door is open, a river of soapy water pours out all over the floor. There is water everywhere and soap bubbles are floating through the air. My goodness! How is Tom going to explain this to Mother Rabbit? Will she understand that he only wanted to rescue his glasses?

April 20

A glasses case

"Mother!" says Tom, hanging his head. "There's something I have to tell you." Oh no, thinks Mother, what has happened now? "I was looking for my glasses, which were in my jeans pocket, and the jeans were in the machine and then...and then..."
"Yes, what happened then?" asks Mother.
"I've lost my glasses!" Mother puts Tom on her lap and says: "Your glasses weren't in the machine. I always empty your pockets first. I found your glasses a long time ago. But do you know what? I'm going to make a glasses case for your glasses. Then you can put them in there when you're playing games outside. That way you won't lose them ever again. Isn't that better?"
"Much better," says Tom.

April 21   Little Red Rabbit Hood

Have you heard that old tale
of little Red Rabbit Hood
and of the fox, who thought she was
a tender, tasty morsel good?
Red Rabbit Hood paid not a thought
to the sly old fox but, rather,
she said: "I'm bringing Granny cakes
deep in the woods, much farther."
"How very sweet," the fox had said,
and yet he had a hunch
that he would get there first and then
would eat them both for lunch!
But then it was that Woodsman Dan
burst in from out the wood.
He beat the fox and so it was
he saved Red Rabbit Hood.

April 22   Fairy tales

The Fluffytails love to hear the fairy tale of Red Rabbit
Hood and the fox. They're so nervous as she walks all alone
through the woods on her way to bring her grandmother
cakes. And afterward, the little rabbits huddle together with
fear when the fox eats up Grandmother and then lies in
Grandmother's bed, waiting for Red Rabbit Hood to
come in. Fortunately, there is always a happy ending.
Wild Woodsman Dan bursts into Grandmother's
cottage and saves Red Rabbit Hood.

April 23

Mirror, mirror on the wall

"Why don't we playact a fairy story?" suggests Daisy Fluffytail. "Great!" say the others. "Which one do you want to do? Red Rabbit Hood?"

"No," says Daisy, "I'd rather do Nose White and the Seven Dwarf Rabbits."

"Oh, and you'll want to be Nose White, of course!" says Hop. "Not at all!" replies Daisy crossly. "I'll be the wicked stepmother."

Hop thinks that it's a bit of a strange choice. Who would want to be the wicked stepmother? But suddenly it all makes sense to her. Nose White's wicked stepmother has a magic mirror! Just look. Daisy is already playing the part. She says: "Mirror, mirror on the wall, who's the fairest of them all?" She doesn't mind that she's the wicked stepmother as long as she can look at herself in the mirror!

April 24

Powder

"You don't have any powder, do you?" Freckle asks Daisy.
"Powder? What do you want powder for?" asks Daisy. She doesn't understand.
"Well," says Freckle, "it's because I hate my freckles so much. I thought that if I had some powder I'd be able to powder my nose and cover them up. A really thick layer of powder so you can't see them anymore." Now Daisy understands. "That's the sort of powder you mean. No, I don't have any." Freckle lets out a deep sigh.
"Then that's the end of my bright idea."
"But we could still ask the others, couldn't we?" Daisy says. Daisy can just imagine how awful she would feel if she was the one with freckles.

April 25

I've had an idea

Freckle and Daisy are looking for some face powder. Freckle needs the face powder to cover up the freckles on her face. They ask all their brothers and sisters if they have any powder. But nobody does. "Gus is the only one we haven't asked yet," sighs Freckle. "But he won't even know what we mean."
"We can still try," says Daisy.
Gus listens very carefully to his sisters' story.
"I don't have any powder either," he says, "but I think I have an idea...." And he chuckles to himself. "Just follow me."

Flour

Gus has had an idea. He's going to help Freckle to get rid of her freckles. That's why he takes her and Daisy into the kitchen. He points to a high-up shelf and says: "There's a bag of flour up there. Why not use some flour as face powder? If you rub it into your cheeks and nose, your freckles will disappear."
Right away, he gets a stool, climbs onto it and reaches for the bag of flour. But, oh dear! the stool begins to wobble and down falls Gus onto the floor. And the bag of flour falls with him, right on his head. He's completely covered in it. He looks just like a ghost! "Well!" says Freckle. "I don't want to end up looking like that!" But because Gus was only trying his best to help, they clean up the mess in the kitchen together.

April 27   Toothache

Hip's right cheek is all big and fat, and Hop's left cheek has swollen up like a balloon as well. Hip and Hop have a toothache. Mrs. Fluffytail calls the dentist at once and makes an appointment. They must be there in an hour.
"Ow! Ow! Ow!" groans Hip. "Ouch! Ooh! Ouch!" moans his sister. To help take away some of the pain, their mother has tied a big handkerchief around their heads. Hip has a red handkerchief with white dots and Hop has a blue one with yellow stripes. A little later, they are at the dentist, sitting in Doctor Bucktooth's waiting room. Very soon, it is their turn to see him. But even though their toothache hurts so much, they are still scared of going to see him. "Come along, children!" says Doctor Bucktooth. "Surely you're not frightened of the dentist?" Well, as a matter of fact, yes, they are!

April 28   Talkative

Dentist Bucktooth has drilled a little hole in Hip and Hop's bad teeth and has given them fillings. Their toothache has gone. "The dentist wasn't scary at all!" says Hip bravely. Mother smiles. Those two are very talkative all of a sudden, she thinks. But when they were at the dentist's it was a rather different story. "And what did Doctor Bucktooth say to you both?" she asks. "To brush our teeth twice a day!" say the twins in chorus. "Well, let's hope that you do!" laughs Mother Rabbit.

April 29

Chattering teeth

Hip and Hop are glad not to have toothaches anymore. From now on, they are very good about brushing their teeth twice a day. They make quite sure that their brothers and sisters do the same as well. "Brush them properly!" they say. "Otherwise you'll get a toothache and you'll have to see the dentist." "But the dentist was very friendly, wasn't he?" says Tom with surprise. "And I thought you said that it wasn't a bit scary," says Roberta. "And that it didn't hurt at all," says Gus. Now the twins will have to be honest. They must admit that they were really scared. Afterward, once it's all over, everything is fine. But when you're waiting there at the dentist's, that's a different thing altogether.

April 30 **Teeth**

Always take care of your teeth and never be in doubt that if you don't, the dentist *might* pull every last one out! You will not ever chew again. You'll suck soup through a straw and eat the same meal every day. Oh, what an awful bore!

May 1   In May...

"How beautifully the birds sing, don't they?" sighs Harry
Fluffytail. "Yes, they really do!" replies his brother Tom.
"It's as if they're singing more beautifully now than usual,"
Harry remarks. "Oh, but they are," says Tom. "Really?
Why is that?" wonders Harry. "It's because they're very
busy at this time of year." "Busy doing what?" asks
Harry. "You really don't know anything, do you?" teases
Tom. "Oh, and I suppose you do!" shouts Harry angrily.
"As a matter of fact, I know lots more than
you do!" "Oh, sure you do, four-eyes, with your
stupid glasses!" The two Fluffytail children are having
a real argument now. They're calling each other all
kinds of unkind names. But suddenly something
stops them. How strange!
It has gone as quiet as night in the wood.
The birds have all stopped
singing.

May 2

Silence

No sound. No noise.
How very odd!
All through the Wild Wood,
there is no birdsong anywhere.
How strange. How far from good.
Or is it strange, I ask myself,
that little birds who sing,
when they hear your screams and
shouts, should tremble and take wing?
Oh, little birds,
please sing again.
We'll fight no more.
We are sorry to cause you pain.

May 3
All birds lay eggs in May

Nervously, Harry and Tom Fluffytail look all around them. Why have the birds stopped singing? Suddenly, they hear an angry voice coming from a tree. Oscar the Owl is sitting on one of its branches. He's looking very cross. "You were screaming and shouting so much that you frightened away all the birds!" he says. "I hope you've finished all that fighting now!" "Yes, Oscar," replies Tom in a shaky voice. "Honestly, we have," says Harry. "But Tom said that I was stupid." "And so you are," replies the owl. "You don't even seem to know that all birds lay their eggs in May. Except for me, of course. I'm much too busy thinking."

May 4   Ears

Perhaps you still remember what very good care all the Fluffytail children take of their tails. They wash them with cold water every morning and brush them until they are all nice and fluffy. As soon as the sun starts to shine, they go and sit with their tails in the sun. Mrs. Fluffytail makes quite sure of it.
"What a big fuss to make about all those little tails," mutters Mr. Fluffytail. He thinks that ears are much more important. "A fluffy tail is nice to look at," he says, "but ears are very useful. You can use your ears to listen for danger." He does have a point there, of course. He has a beautiful pair of ears himself. They're so large that he must be able to hear a very long way indeed!

May 5   Ear splints

Father Fluffytail has very good ears and he's extremely proud of them. That's why he's not so very happy that Gus has such floppy ears. "You can't possibly hear properly with ears like that," he sighs. "Oh, it's all right, really," says Gus, trying to comfort him. "It isn't at all," says Father Rabbit decisively. "So, we'd better do something about those ears of yours right away." He takes Gus along with him to his workshop. He picks four little sticks that are nice and straight, and then uses them to hold Gus's ears upright by tying some bandages around them. The sticks are just like splints for a broken arm. "So," he says, "can you hear me better now?" Gus doesn't reply. He can sees his father's mouth move, but because of the bandages wrapped around his ears he can't hear a thing.

May 6   Blindfolded

"I really *can* hear perfectly well," Gus Fluffytail tells his father. Father Fluffytail looks at him with concern. He doesn't quite believe him. "Do you know what?" he suggests. "We'll have a little competition. We'll both put on a blindfold and ask Mother to make a noise. The winner is the first to guess what that noise is." Mrs. Fluffytail goes and stands a good distance away from them. Gus and his father put on their blindfolds. They both listen hard. Then Gus says: "Mother's taking something out of her pocket!" Father rabbit can't believe it. "Is that true?" he asks. He hadn't heard a thing himself. "Yes, it's true," laughs Mother. "Even with those floppy ears of his, Gus can hear much better than you can!"

May 7   Red alert

"Red alert!" calls out Leaper Fluffytail. "Red alert!"
His brothers and sisters come running to see what it is that's
happened. "Somebody has dug up our whole soccer field!"
Leaper tells them. Leaper loves playing soccer. He's quite
happy doing nothing else all day long. He practices playing
soccer on the grass from dawn until dusk if he can.
But when he went to the soccer field this morning
there was very little grass left to see. It looked
just like a plowed field. Instead of grass,
Leaper saw only earth, earth, and
more earth. "Someone has definitely
been up to no good. Someone really
mean who likes to play pranks on
rabbit children," says Leaper angrily.

May 8   Rabbit prankster

"There's a rabbit prankster in the wood!"
the Fluffytail children tell their father.
Father Fluffytail scratches behind his ear.
"A rabbit prankster? What's going on?"
"Just come and look, Father!" shouts
Leaper. "The rabbit prankster has ruined
our soccer field!" Father Fluffytail goes to
look at once. When he sees the field he
can't stop himself from laughing. Leaper
can't believe his eyes. Why does his father
think it's so funny? He's about to march
off in a temper when Father Rabbit puts
a paw on his son's shoulder and says:
"That prankster of yours didn't mean to
upset you at all! It's Montague Mole. He
has such bad eyesight that he can't tell
the difference between a soccer
and a toadstool. Come along
now. We'll go and pay him
a visit."

May 9   Montague Mole

Father Fluffytail hops over to a large molehill and calls down below: "Hello, Montague! Are you at home?" A few moments later, they hear a faint scrabbling sound. A couple of lumps of earth fly out of the hole in the molehill and all at once, there he is: Montague Mole.

"Who is it?" he asks, talking to a tree. Montague has such bad eyesight that he thinks that the tree trunk is one of the forest animals.

"It's us. Father and Leaper Fluffytail." "Ah, yes indeed, so I see," says the mole, staring at two big stones in the ground. "Mr. Mole, would it be possible for you to do your digging a little further away?" asks Father Fluffytail politely. "It's just that this is my children's soccer field."

"Oh, indeed! But of course! So sorry! I didn't know anything about a soccer field," says Montague Mole to his own feet. "I'll get on with it right away. Indeed I will!" Once he has gone underground again, Leaper is able to laugh about it. The poor old mole couldn't help his mistake, after all.

May 10

Secrets

It's nearly Mother Rabbit's birthday. The Fluffytail children are all being very secretive. Each one has thought of a surprise for Mother, but none of them will tell the others what the surprise is. "What are you going to do?" Daisy asks Charlie.
"I'm not telling," replies Charlie. "It's a secret."
"But you can tell me, can't you?" says Daisy, trying one more time. "It's not as if I was Mother." "No, but if I tell you then you'll only copy what I do," says Charlie knowingly. "No, I won't. I have an idea of my own that's much better than yours anyway." "What are you going to do?" "If you're not going to tell me what you're doing, then I'm not going to tell you what I'm doing either," says Daisy, going off in a sulk.

May 11

Very early

Daisy wakes up very early in the morning. She slips very quietly outside. Nobody must hear her because today is her mother's birthday. Daisy wants to surprise Mother Fluffytail. She's going to pick a big bunch of flowers for her. She could have done it the day before, of course, but her brothers and sisters would have seen it. And then they would simply have copied her. That's not at all what Daisy wants. It's her own idea, and hers alone. And in any case, flowers are at their best when you pick them first thing in the morning. That's why Daisy creeps out of bed so very early. She knows a spot where the loveliest flowers grow. It's an open glade in the woods. I'd better hurry, thinks Daisy, otherwise I won't be home when Mother gets up.

May 12   The same idea

Daisy Fluffytail trips quickly through the wood. She's off to pick a bunch of flowers for her mother's birthday. But wait a moment. Whatever is going on? As Daisy reaches the woodland glade she sees ten pairs of little rabbit ears sticking out from among all the flowers: nine little pairs of perky ears and one pair of droopy ones. All the Fluffytail children have had the same idea. They have all gone to the woodland glade this morning. At first, Daisy is very disappointed, but she soon sees the funny side. Then, along with the others, she helps to pick the biggest bouquet of flowers in the world.

May 13   Flowers

The Fluffytail children giggle as they go to their parents' bedroom. Their arms are filled with flowers. And because there are eleven of them, that means an awful lot of flowers indeed.

"Good morning, Mother!" they all shout. "Happy birthday!" And then they throw all the flowers onto their mother's bed. There are so many that you can't see the bedcovers any more. You can only see Mother's face poking through all the flowers. "What beautiful flowers!" she exclaims, overcome with surprise and happiness.

May 14

How strange!

Mrs. Fluffytail is looking for Freckle. How strange! Freckle is usually busy doing something somewhere indoors. She always helps Mother with chores in the home. But just when Mrs. Fluffytail wants to fold up the bedsheets, Freckle is nowhere to be found. And she can't possibly fold up those big sheets all by herself!
Oh well, in that case she'll just have to ask Billy.
"Billy, would you help me for a moment with the sheets?" she calls.
"Yes, Mother, I'm coming!" says Billy obediently. He takes hold of the sheet, but does so a little clumsily. Before you know it, the sheet has fallen on the floor. It's covered in dirty marks!
"Sorry, Mother!" says Billy. "It's better to ask Freckle to help with this sort of thing than me."
"I know," says Mrs. Fluffytail, "but Freckle has disappeared. I can't find her!" Billy thinks it's very strange as well.

May 15   Cobweb

Freckle Fluffytail hasn't disappeared. She simply doesn't feel like working today. "Let the others help out for once!" she says. "I'm going off to read a nice book in the sunshine." She has found herself a quiet spot underneath an old tree where she can read her book. Freckle is soon so deep into her book that she doesn't notice Stella the Spider dropping down toward her from a tree branch. Stella looks at Freckle's long ears and, because Freckle isn't moving the slightest bit, Stella thinks: Oh, that would make a good spot for my web. She starts at once to spin the most beautiful web between Freckle's ears. Billy just happens to hop by later on, and can't stop himself from laughing when he sees Freckle. "Freckle," he says, "with all those cobwebs in between your ears you're much better off cleaning than reading!"

May 16

A lazy day

Today I'm going to linger.
I will not lift a finger!
I owe myself just one free day
to yawn and stretch and maybe play.
Today I will have fun
and lie back in the sun.
Today's the day that I am boss.
I won't get tired. I won't get
cross. Today I'll spend
with ease just doing
as I please!

May 17

Shock

Hip and Hop Fluffytail want to know whether or not they have grown any bigger. So Father Fluffytail has put a tape measure on the wall on which there is a marker that can slide up and down. All that the Fluffytail children have to do is to stand with their backs to it and then slide down the marker until it touches their heads. Then they can turn around and see how tall they are. It's Hip's turn first. Hip measures seven inches, which is really quite big for a rabbit. "Your turn, Hop," says Hip. But when Hop looks at the tape measure it shows that she measures eight inches. What a shock. "Now we're not really twins anymore!" cries Hip. And worse still is that, of the two of them, he is the shortest. He thinks that girls are the ones who should be shorter.

May 18

Rain in May

Hip is angry. Angry that Hop is taller than him. The tape measure said a whole inch taller. "Do you know what you should do?" says Hop to Hip. "If you want to grow taller, you should go and stand in the rain because the rain in May makes you grow." Hip doesn't really look like he believes her but, even so, he does go off to stand in the rain later on. If I stand here for long enough, I'll be able to catch up with Hop, he thinks. He's still standing there an hour later. His clothes are soaking wet and every now and then, he lets out a very loud sneeze. "That's quite enough!" Hop calls out to her brother. "Let's measure ourselves again!"

May 19

Not surprising

Once again, Hip and Hop Fluffytail stand against the tape measure on the wall. Hip is hoping that he has grown since he last measured himself. He wants to be at least as tall as his sister Hop, if not taller. After all, he didn't go stand in the May rain for nothing. "Just stand still for a moment!" shouts Hop. She can't put the tape measure's sliding marker in the right place because Hip keeps on sneezing. "Ah...ah...ah...tchooo!" sneezes Hip. "Have I grown any more?"

"No," sighs Hop, "I'm still taller than you are." "Maybe you didn't measure me right," says Hip. "Go and stand next to the tape measure again." Hop does as he asks. And then Hip suddenly sees what has happened. He's not shorter than Hop at all! But Hop has kept her shoes on. It's not surprising that she seemed to be taller! And he'd been standing in the pouring rain for a whole hour all because of that!

May 20

Jump roping

"One! Two! Jump right through. Three! Four! Jump once more!" sing Daisy and Freckle Fluffytail.
They're happily playing with their jump rope. And Gus is helping to turn the rope around. Daisy and Freckle never mind that Gus helps. There needs to be two of you to turn a jump rope, but because Gus just turns it and doesn't jump means that Daisy and Freckle can both take turns jumping in and out of the rope. "With my funny ears I wouldn't be very good at jumping anyway," says Gus. Daisy and Freckle don't think that's such a bad thing, howeewer. They like jumping much more than turning the rope.

May 21

Do you want to play too?

Daisy and Freckle are having great fun. They're jumping with their jump rope, and it's going really well today. Look! Here comes Leaper. "Do you want to play too, Leaper?" asks Freckle. "If you do, you can take my place. I'm feeling a bit tired." "Thanks," says Leaper, and with a few little hops, he jumps perfectly through the rope. Leaper is extremely good at games. The jump rope is as easy as falling off a log to him. He jumps and skips and never steps on the rope. "Gosh, Leaper! You're much too good at this," says Daisy. "At this rate we'll never get our turn!" "What? Oh, I'm sorry!" pants Leaper.
"Now you can go again, and I'll help turn the rope."

May 22   Silly girls' game

"Do you want to jump too?" Daisy asks her sister Roberta. She means to be friendly, but Roberta sticks her nose in the air. She likes rough boys' games more.

"A jump rope? Ugh! That's just a silly girls' game. I'm not doing that," she says. But Leaper doesn't agree with her. "Didn't you know," he says, "that nearly everyone in sports does jump roping? It's very good for you. And once you get good at jumping, you find your energy lasts even longer playing other games."

Roberta still isn't totally sure. "It's true, sis, honest," says Leaper. "I do it too because I want to have strong muscles."

Oh my, Roberta is surprised.

May 23

Snail

Harry Fluffytail plays such terrible practical jokes. This morning, he frightened his mother really badly. While she was hanging out the washing on the line, she took a clothespin from the basket and found that it wasn't a clothespin at all, but a very large snail. It's not that she's afraid of snails, but if you've ever touched one you'll know it's still a nasty, slimy feeling all the same. Mrs. Fluffytail was so startled and so cross that she went to fetch the carpet beater from the kitchen. She knew exactly who it was who had played that trick on her. "Harry Fluffytail!" she called out. "You just wait and see what you get when I catch you!" That made Harry really scared and he crept away as quietly as a mouse.

May 24

No more practical jokes

There he is. Harry Fluffytail is hopping slowly through the wood, all alone. He doesn't dare go home just yet. He's played such a nasty joke on his mother that he's better off staying out of her way for a while. Harry doesn't know why he teases people so much. It just happens that way. Ideas keep coming up in his head. And before you know it, he's put a frog in Daisy's bed or tied the laces of Gus's shoes together. Only later does Harry realize that the others don't think his little jokes are at all funny. But then it's far too late! "From now on I won't play any more practical jokes on anyone!" he promises.

May 25

How funny

Harry Fluffytail is whistling cheerfully to himself as he hops on through the wood. He's forgotten all about how cross his mother was with him. He's also forgotten that he promised never to play any more practical jokes. Suddenly, he sees something reddish behind a bush. Very carefully, he goes over to take a look and sees Rusty the Fox who is lying there all curled up, in the sunshine. All at once, a twinkle comes into Harry's eyes. As long as the fox sleeps, he has time to think of a trick to play on him. Harry creeps closer on tiptoe. He ties the fox's tail to the bush with a strong piece of string. Once he has tied ten knots in the string, he runs around and around the fox, shouting: "Try and catch me if you can!" Rusty wakes up with a start, sees the rabbit, takes a great leap...and stays exactly where he was!
His tail is tied firmly to the bush. Harry laughs until he thinks he's going to burst. But didn't Harry say he was going to stop playing practical jokes?

103

May 26 Flute

Billy Fluffytail has made a flute from a reed. He could have made a recorder, but a flute is easier for him to play because rabbits have such big front teeth. Billy would have bitten a recorder to pieces with his big teeth.

"What beautiful music, Billy," sighs his sister Roberta. "I wish I could play like that."

"Oh, but you can," says Billy.

"Don't be so silly. I wouldn't know how I'm supposed to blow on a flute like that. And then having to keep all those little holes covered with my paws! It's much too difficult!" complains Roberta.

Billy plays a little tune on his flute. "But there are other instruments you can play as well, you know," he says.

"But they don't sound as nice as your flute," argues Roberta.

"They sound different. But if you played something at the same time as me, my flute music would sound even more beautiful," explains Billy.

"In that case I'd like one of those other instruments," decides Roberta.

104

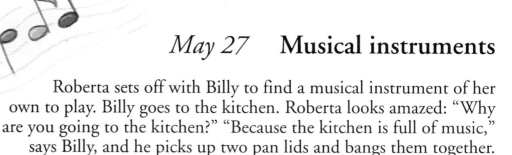

May 27 **Musical instruments**

Roberta sets off with Billy to find a musical instrument of her own to play. Billy goes to the kitchen. Roberta looks amazed: "Why are you going to the kitchen?" "Because the kitchen is full of music," says Billy, and he picks up two pan lids and bangs them together. Crash! Crash! "Oh no!" says Roberta, "I don't like that sound at all." "What about this then?" asks Billy, and he hits a bucket with two wooden spoons. "No, I don't like that either." "Wait!" says Billy. "I know what." He gets ten empty bottles and fills them with water. He fills the first one completely full, and all the others with a little bit less water each time. Then he taps against them with a spoon. Each bottle makes a different sound. "You can play all kinds of tunes with this," he says. "Yes," agrees Roberta, "that sounds lovely."

May 28 **Orchestra**

Roberta and Billy are playing music together. Billy is playing the flute and Roberta is playing on her bottles. The other Fluffytails hear how good it sounds. "Can we play too?" they ask. Of course they can. Even so, it's quite a problem finding them all an instrument to play. Leaper chooses the pan lids and Harry chooses the bucket drum. Something special has been chosen for Daisy: a musical comb. Billy has folded a piece of tissue paper over the comb. Daisy can use her lips on the comb to make a humming noise. Hip and Hop both have a can filled with pebbles that they can shake about to their hearts' content. Tom can blow through an old piece of garden hose: "Peep! Peep!" Freckle rubs a clothespin up and down an old washboard: "Grrrt! Grrrt!" Charlie has found an old car horn: "Toot! Toot!" And Gus rings his bicycle bell: "Ding! Ding!"

May 29 **Tidying up**

Charlie Fluffytail must tidy up. All kinds of things are lying on the floor that he has just dropped there. Mother Fluffytail has had enough of it. "You're to tidy up that mess now, Charlie!" she said. "You can't come to sit at the table until it's finished." She really means it, and so Charlie sets to work right away. Charlie isn't really untidy, but whenever he's playing with something he can suddenly feel terribly tired. Before you know it, he's shut his eyes and falls asleep there on the spot. By the time he wakes up again, he's forgotten whatever it was he was playing with before. Then he just starts playing with something else. Charlie can hardly believe that he has made all this mess all by himself. His wooden train set is out of its box and lying on the floor, half put together. A jigsaw puzzle is sticking out from underneath a pile of books and his bowling pins are all jumbled up in the corner. It makes Charlie tired just looking at it all. Does he really have to tidy up all of that?

May 30   Shhh!

Mother Fluffytail wonders what's keeping Charlie so long. He was supposed to tidy up his toys before dinnertime. But now, everyone has cleaned their plates and Charlie still hasn't come downstairs. So she decides to take a look. When she opens the playroom door, she sees all the books standing neatly on the bookshelves. The toy train is in its box and all the building blocks have been tidied up. The bowling pins are all standing in a row with the ball next to them. In fact, the room looks as good as new. But where is Charlie? Then mother rabbit sees him. Charlie has fallen asleep in the corner along with the cuddly toys and dolls. He was so tired from tidying up that he couldn't keep his eyes open any longer. There he lies, snoring, on top of a rag doll. Very quietly, Mother closes the door again. Let him have a good sleep, she thinks, because she knows how very much Charlie likes sleeping. Missing his meal just this once won't do him any harm.

May 31   Sleepyhead

Our Charlie's such a sleepyhead.
Just see him stretch and yawn in bed,
his eyes filled with the magic dust
the Sandman brought, so sleep he must.
"It's really late and time for bed,"
the Sun says as he's turning red.
"That he sleeps well, I hope and pray.
Tomorrow is another day."
But Charlie is so tired that his eyes are
shut shut tight as they can be.
He won't be staying long awake.
A trip to dreamland he must make.

June 1 Punished?

"Wonderful! What splendid weather!" exclaims
Father Fluffytail that morning. He looks outside,
does a big, long stretch, and dashes off to the
kitchen at once.
The Fluffytail children are all awake. Even inside
their little hole under the ground they can feel that
it's going to be a lovely day. They're all in a great
rush at breakfast. They want to be outside so much
that they almost drink up their porridge. It goes
down the wrong way for little Gus, and Freckle, his
big sister, has to pat him on the back for five
minutes before he's better. Only then is he able to
breathe properly again. "Wait here for just a while
once you've finished your porridge," says Father
Fluffytail. "Oh, Father! That's not fair!" they all call
out. "We want to go outside!" They don't
understand it. Why do they have to stay at the
table? Are they being punished for something?

June 2 Some more to eat?

The Fluffytail children are sitting at the breakfast table
with long faces. They emptied their bowls ages ago.
But Father has told them that they must wait there. "I
think it's mean," grumbles Harry. "Just when the
weather is nice, we're punished. And what for?
I haven't done anything!" Father Fluffytail chuckles
to himself, but doesn't say a word. From the
kitchen, he takes some knives, butter, bread
and jam, and puts them on the breakfast
table. The little rabbits can't imagine what
their father's up to. Haven't they just
had their porridge? Do they have to
have breakfast all over again? "I really
can't eat any more, father! Just so
you know," whines Leaper. Father
can't keep the joke to himself any
longer. He bursts out laughing.
He has fooled his children.

June 3   Picnic

Father Fluffytail has just played a trick on his
children. He fooled them into thinking that they
had to stay indoors as some kind of punishment.
And just when the weather outside was so
beautiful too!
"Don't worry," he says, "none of you is being
punished for anything. But if we all start to
butter some of this bread for a picnic...."
He doesn't need to speak another word.
"Hooray! We're going to go on a picnic!" shout
eleven little rabbits all at once. And in no time at all,
a big heap of sandwiches is ready on the table.

June 4   A Walk

The Fluffytail family are going off to the wood
for a picnic. They're all carrying backpacks.
There are sandwiches and drinks inside.
They're going to have their picnic in the
meadow. It's fabulous weather. The wood
looks both beautiful and mysterious all at the
same time. "It looks just like an enchanted
forest," says Daisy. "You'd better watch
out!" Harry teases her. "There's a witch
standing behind that big tree and she's
going to get you!" "Oh, don't be so
silly!" replies Daisy. But as she goes
past the big, old tree she does
glance behind herself, even so.

June 5

The enchanted forest

Rustling trees here talk in secret.
Babbling murmurs from the
stream. Use your ears and hear
soft voices. Is it real or all a dream?
Hidden 'midst the tangled bushes,
in the forest's heart so deep, there
are elves who play, and also trolls
who through the shadows creep.
Dwarfs are busy painting toadstools. Red with around little
white dots. Witches throw toads
in their cauldrons, making potions
that cause spots. Be on your guard
and listen well wherever it is darkest.
You just can't tell what might jump
out in the Enchanted Forest.

June 6 Feeling

frightened

It's a little bit dark between the trees
on either side of the path the
Fluffytail family are following. Father
and Mother Fluffytail can't help quietly
chuckling to themselves about their
children. The little rabbits have such
imaginations! Behind every tree they see
witches or dragons. Just imagine if there
was a troll nearby. The Fluffytail children
tell each other the scariest of stories. They
love to be a little bit frightened. Daisy is
the only one who thinks it's all far too
frightening. She walks between
her father and mother.

June 7 Scared

Mrs. Fluffytail feels sorry for Daisy. Her brothers and sisters have been telling each other scary stories. They were so horrible that Daisy quickly sandwiched herself in between her mother and father. The others are capering about the dark woods from one side of the path to the other.
"You know, we shouldn't really let the children frighten Daisy so much," says Mrs. Fluffytail to her husband. "Oh, it's all right," he replies. "They're really just as scared as she is. But as long as they're scared they'll be on the lookout for danger. Deep inside, they know very well that there aren't any witches. But just suppose that Rusty the Fox should be behind one of the trees. Then at least they'll be expecting something."

June 8 The meadow

After a long journey, the Fluffytail family finally arrives at the meadow. Daisy at once dives in among all the poppies and forget-me-nots. How happy she feels to be out of that dark, scary wood at last. "Where are the others?" asks Mrs. Fluffytail worriedly. "Surely they'll be thirsty after coming such a long way." "Don't get upset, my dear," says Mr. Fluffytail. "They'll be here for sure when they're thirsty enough." Then he closes his eyes for forty winks.

June 9   The picnic quilt

Daisy is picking flowers while the other children are exploring. Meanwhile, Mother Rabbit is getting the picnic ready. She takes a big, special quilt out of her backpack. The quilt was made by her very own great-grandmother. Everyone has always been very careful with it. It has only ever been used for picnics. That's why it still looks so very nice even though it's very old. Mrs. Fluffytail's great-grandmother could sew beautifully. She sewed together many different little bits and pieces of cloth. So many, in fact, that she ended up making a huge quilt in the shape of the sun with a happy, smiling face.

June 10

Hungry!

Helter-skelter, ten little rabbits come tumbling into the meadow. As soon as they see the heap of sandwiches on the picnic quilt, they want to start gobbling them up right away. "Just a minute!" says Father Fluffytail. "First wash your hands." Luckily, there's a little stream nearby. The little Fluffytails quickly dip their paws in the cool water. And then it's helter-skelter all the way back to the sandwiches. In a flash, all the sandwiches have gone. The eleven Fluffytail children are now all lying on the picnic quilt, their tummies bulging.

June 11   **Back home**

The Fluffytail family has been in the meadow all day long.
They've had a wonderful picnic and have played all kinds of lively
games. But now it's time to go back home. The sun is already low
in the sky. If they are to be home before dark they will have to
hurry. They quickly pack up their backpacks. "Ah!" sighs Gus
Fluffytail contentedly. "Now that we've eaten up all the
sandwiches my backpack doesn't feel so heavy anymore."
"Is everyone ready?" asks Father Rabbit, and he counts
their fluffy tails to see if they are all there. "There's
Freckle and Gus, Tom and Leaper, Roberta and the
twins, Daisy and Billy, Harry and...Charlie!
Where is Charlie?" cries out Father in alarm.

June 12   **Searching**

Where has Charlie Fluffytail gone? The whole
Fluffytail family searches and searches, but
Charlie can't be found anywhere.
"Where can my little Charlie have gone to?"
sniffs Mrs. Fluffytail with tears in her eyes. "It's
beginning to get dark and the children have to be
in bed."
"Yes," nods Father Rabbit, "and it's a very long way
home as well."
He thinks long and hard. Then he says: "My dear, you
must go home with the smallest children. If you hurry,
you'll be home before dark. I'll stay here and search with
Harry and Freckle. Don't you worry about a thing.
We'll find him!"

June 13

Heavy

Wiping her eyes, Mrs. Fluffytail turns around. Oh well, I'd better get going, she thinks. She goes over to her backpack and tries to pick it up. Oomph! Goodness, that's heavy! Perhaps Harry has put a stone in it as a joke. She opens the backpack and takes out the picnic quilt. She can feel that whatever it is that makes it so heavy is inside the quilt. She unrolls it, and what do you think she finds? Charlie! Mrs. Fluffytail is overjoyed and cross all at the same time. If she hadn't noticed, they might have been looking for Charlie for ages!

June 14   **Nightfall**

It is now very late because of all the time it took to find Charlie. "Keep going, children!" says Father Fluffytail, pushing his big family onward. He wants to get them home before nightfall. Once night does fall, it will be very dark and dangerous for rabbits in the wood. That's when Rusty the Fox goes out hunting! "I'm so tired!" complains Hop, and her twin brother, Hip, can hardly keep on his feet anymore. "Just a little farther. We're almost there!" At last they are home. What a day!

June 15 Footprints

The Fluffytail family has been away for the whole day. That's why they know nothing about all the commotion that's going on at Rabbit Hill. The whole rabbit warren is in an uproar. Their neighbor, Mr. Longears, comes to fetch Father Fluffytail. "Are you coming to the meeting?" "Meeting? Why is there a meeting?" asks Mr. Fluffytail. "Haven't you heard the news?" asks Mr. Longears, astonished. "Strange footprints have been found, right next to Rabbit Hill." "What sort of footprints? Not Rusty the Fox, surely?" says Father Fluffytail, shocked. "No, they're very unusual footprints. Nobody has ever seen anything like them before!" explains the neighbor. Harry Fluffytail has been secretly listening to the conversation. "I'll bet they're a fire-breathing dragon's footprints," he tells his brothers and sisters. They cover up their eyes in fright.

June 16

Dragon

The dragon roars
and fiery flames he spits
shoot from
his snout in fits.
His great, razor-sharp set of teeth
are cruel and heartless white.
His spiky tail now lashes forth
with all its furious might.
His long, curved claws have made their mark.
Deep footprints in the sand.
Such footprints can mean but one thing:
"A dragon's in the land!"

June 17

A meeting

Father Fluffytail and all the other rabbit fathers from Rabbit Hill are having a meeting. Strange footprints have been found right next to their rabbit holes. Footprints of a kind that nobody has ever seen before.

Archibald Graypaw, the oldest rabbit, scratches his chin. "My fellow rabbits," he says, "we are gathered together because of a most serious matter. Those strange footprints may mean danger to us. Naturally, they cannot belong to a dragon because dragons do not exist. But to whom *do* they belong? Nobody knows. And so, each one of us will take turns to keep a night watch." The rabbit fathers all nod. It's a good plan. "I'll be the first to keep watch tonight," offers Father Fluffytail. He *is* a brave rabbit, isn't he? Nearly as brave as Wild Woodsman Dan!

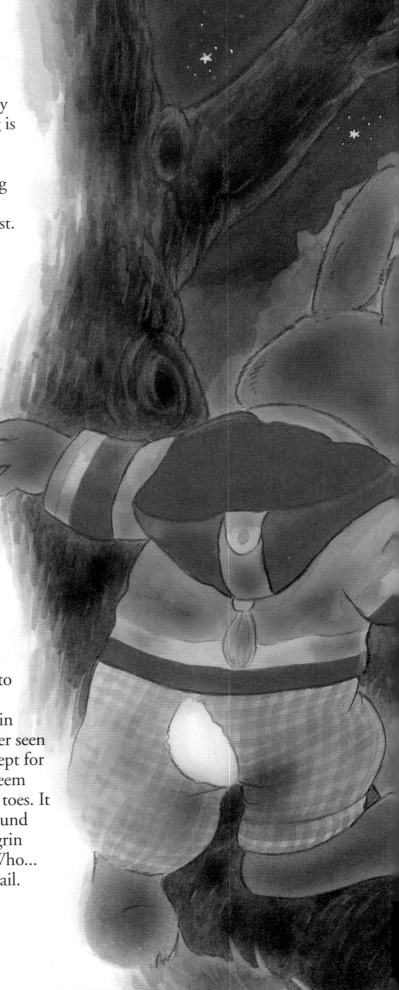

June 18   The night-watch

The rabbits of Rabbit Hill are nervous. They
have the feeling that someone or something is
sneaking around their neighborhood. They
have found strange footprints. The rabbit
fathers have decided to take turns at keeping
watch by night. Tonight, it's Father Fluffytail's turn. As soon as it's dark, he's at his post.
He keeps his ears and eyes well open. He
acted very bravely about it in front of his
children. They think he's as brave as Wild
Woodsman Dan. But deep in his heart,
Father Fluffytail is scared too. "Hey! Who
goes there?" calls out Father Fluffytail,
startled. He hears some twigs crack.
"Tee-hee-hee!" comes a sound. Father
Fluffytail soon forgets his fear. He's
being laughed at! He angrily calls out
into the night: "Come and show
yourself, if you dare!"

June 19   A strange creature

Father Fluffytail is angry. Someone is
laughing at him! And that someone is
hiding somewhere in the dark. Father
Fluffytail flashes his light all around but
can't find anything. Could it be that he
imagined it all? Then he hears more twigs
cracking. Right away, he turns the light onto
the bushes. That's where the noise came
from. A very strange creature now appears in
the beam of light. Father Fluffytail has never seen
such an animal. It has dark brown hair except for
its snout, which is bald. Its arms and legs seem
long and lanky, and it has long fingers and toes. It
also has a long, thin tail. It's looking all around
with its saucy brown eyes. And a cheerful grin
turns up the corners of its wide mouth. "Who...
who...who are you?" stutters Father Fluffytail.
"My name's Coco. Coco the Monkey!"

118

June 20   Monkey

Did you ever see such things?
Well, call me carrot head!
Father Rabbit shuts his eyes
and counts to ten instead.
But when he opens them again,
he sees to his great surprise
the beast still standing there. It grins,
a twinkle in its eyes.

"My name is Coco," says the beast.
"The circus I have fled."
But Father Rabbit understands
not much of what he's said.
"I come from far-off Africa,"
explains the ape with grace.
"All monkeys sport a long, thin tail,
and have a saucy face."

June 21   Runaway

Father Fluffytail needs time to calm
down after such a big surprise. He has
never seen a monkey before. Strange
creatures like that do not live in the Wild Wood.
Even so, the animal does look friendly.
"Hello, Coco," he says to the monkey. "What are you
doing in our wood?"
"I've run away," explains Coco. "I was imprisoned by
people. I had to perform all kinds of tricks in the
circus. Every day, over and over again. I'd had enough.
That's why I escaped as soon as I had the chance. I
had to walk a long way. My hands and feet are still
sore."
"You escaped from *people*?" gasps Father Fluffytail.
"We don't like people either. You can stay here
with us for as long as you like!"

June 22

The more, the merrier

Father Fluffytail has brought Coco the Monkey home
with him. Coco has escaped from human beings.
"Come and live with us," says Father Fluffytail to Coco.
"How very kind of you. Are you sure it's no trouble?" asks
Coco.
"Not at all," replies Mr. Fluffytail. "If you already have
eleven children then there's always room for an extra one."
"Eleven children?" Coco can't believe his ears. "Then I'll
bet it's always fun at your house."
"If you like it crowded..." chuckles Mr.
Fluffytail.
"I *do*!" laughs Coco. "When I lived with
people I was stuck all day long in a cage.
I didn't have anyone to talk to.
Having eleven children all around
me sounds just wonderful."

June 23

Chatterboxes

The new guest is an enormous success with the
Fluffytail children. At first they do look at him rather
suspiciously. They have, of course, never seen a monkey
before. But they soon realize that Coco is friendly. "Where do
you come from?" asks Harry.
"I come from a circus made by people," replies Coco.
"What's a circus?" asks Freckle. She has never heard of such a
thing. "A circus is a very big tent," explains Coco. "In the
afternoons and evenings, a whole lot of people come to the
tent. They pay to be allowed in. For that money, the circus
people and animals perform tricks."
"What sort of tricks?" asks Leaper.
"My! My! What a lot of questions you all ask!"
laughs Coco. "What a family of chatterboxes!"

June 24   Circus tricks

"I'll show all of you what sort of tricks I had to do," says Coco the Monkey. The Fluffytail children clap with excitement. They're very curious about what Coco did in the circus.
"I'll need five little balls," says Coco.
"I have a soccer ball," says Leaper.
"Me too!" shouts out Roberta.
"No, those are far too big! I need the sort that I can catch with one hand," sighs Coco.
No, the Fluffytail children aren't able to help. Oh dear, what a shame. They had been so looking forward to one of Coco's tricks.
Then Mrs. Fluffytail asks: "Would it work just as well with balls of wool?"
Coco nods. That's a good idea. A little later, he is juggling with five balls of wool. Goodness, Coco's really good at it!

June 25   Practice

"May I try too?" asks Gus Fluffytail. He's been watching Coco the Monkey juggling the balls of wool. "Of course," says Coco, and he gives Gus the woollen balls.
"At first, just try using two of them."
Gus takes a red ball and a blue one. But however hard he tries, he keeps dropping one or other of them.
"Keep on practicing!" says Coco.
Gus goes to the kitchen. He can practice there in peace. An hour later, Coco goes to take a look at how Gus is doing. But it's still not going so well. The balls of wool have unraveled from all the juggling practice. Only Gus's ears can still be seen from underneath a huge knotted heap of blue and red threads.

June 26 Homesick

Coco the Monkey has been staying with the Fluffytail family for a week now. He enjoys his new, free life for the first few days. He plays games with the eleven Fluffytail children and he swings through the trees in the wood.

But after a while, Coco becomes quieter and quieter. He doesn't laugh as much as before and sometimes he sits leaning against a tree trunk for hours. One day, Mrs. Fluffytail goes up to Coco and gently says: "There's something the matter, isn't there?"

Coco nods. Some little tears are welling up in his dark brown eyes. "You have all been so kind to me," he begins, "and I don't want to upset you, but..."

"I think I can understand what it is," comforts Mrs. Fluffytail. "You're missing your old life."

"Yes, I miss the circus and the children's applause," sighs Coco. "I'm homesick."

June 27
Clever Tom

Coco the Monkey is homesick. "I miss the children's smiling faces," he says. "I made a lot of people very happy with my tricks. And I miss the applause!"

"But we clap for you too!" cries Roberta.

"Yes, and I think it's very sweet of you all," laughs Coco, "but if you're used to a hundred people clapping for you, then eleven little rabbits doesn't seem like very much."

"So, do you want to go back again?" asks Harry Fluffytail.

Coco nods, and then sighs. "But the circus is sure to have moved on by now, and I have no idea where." He starts to sob with sadness. It's really terrible when you feel homesick and you know you can't go back." Luckily, that clever Tom Fluffytail has been listening. "I have a plan!" he cries. "Let's ask the birds if they can find out where the circus is. You can see a long way from high in the sky!"

June 28   Bye-bye, Coco!

"Cooo, cooo!" Wanda the Wood Pigeon listens carefully to Tom Fluffytail. Tom tells her that Coco the Monkey misses the circus. And also that Coco no longer knows where the circus is. "Please, could you fly around for us and find the circus from the air?" asks Tom politely. The fat wood pigeon flutters her eyes and coos: "What is a monkey, and what is a circus?" Tom patiently explains. Afterward, Wanda asks Tom: "And do they travel around in great wagons drawn by horses? If they do, then I already know where the circus is. Quite close by. One of the wagons has a broken wheel. They're repairing it and the other wagons are waiting." What a piece of luck! Tom goes to tell Coco the good news at once. And then the whole Fluffytail family takes Coco to the place where the circus wagons are standing. "Good-bye, Coco!" they call, waving as the wagons set off again. "Bye-bye, Coco! Good luck!"

June 29 **Dreams**

Coco the Monkey stayed with them for a whole week and now he is gone. Perhaps forever. All the Fluffytail children miss the jolly little monkey. But Gus Fluffytail misses him most of all. Coco taught him how to juggle properly. Now, at long last, Gus can do something that the others can't. He has always been the clumsy one in the family. But now, as far as juggling is concerned, he's better than everyone. And he has Coco to thank for that.
"If only I could tell Coco how grateful I am," mumbles Gus to himself.
But Coco is back with the circus again, of course.
Perhaps...just perhaps..., dreams Gus, if I practice very hard, I will also be in the circus when I'm grown up. And then, when people start clapping after I finish my tricks, I'll make a very low bow. So low, my ears will touch the ground.

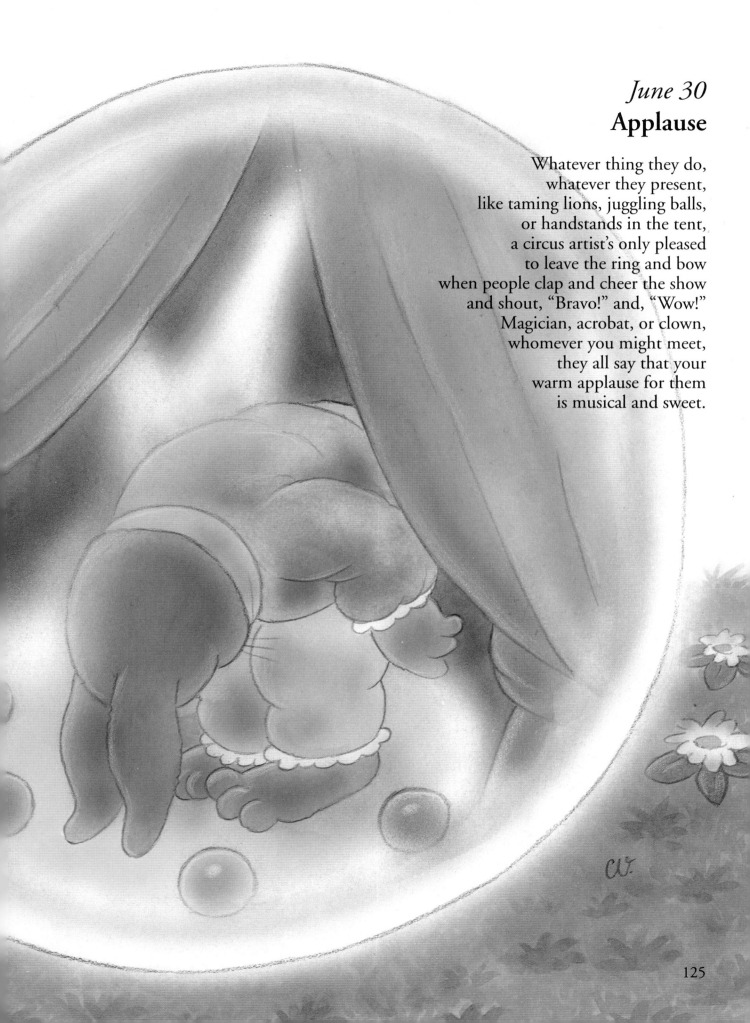

June 30
Applause

Whatever thing they do,
whatever they present,
like taming lions, juggling balls,
or handstands in the tent,
a circus artist's only pleased
to leave the ring and bow
when people clap and cheer the show
and shout, "Bravo!" and, "Wow!"
Magician, acrobat, or clown,
whomever you might meet,
they all say that your
warm applause for them
is musical and sweet.

125

July 1

Patience

Freckle leaves home very early each morning. She's going to a very special place in the woods. Freckle can find it with her eyes shut because she's been there so many times before. The path leads uphill to where big bushes and tall pine trees grow.

Between the pine trees, much smaller plants are growing very close to the ground. They have shiny green leaves and the purest white flowers with yellow centers. If you have the patience to wait long enough, those centers will change into wild strawberries. And Freckle can wait a very long time. That's why Freckle is able to pick the very first strawberry of the whole year. Mmmm, how delicious!

July 2

Baskets full

Freckle Fluffytail has found out that the wild strawberries are ripe. The first one she tastes is deliciously sweet, just like a wild strawberry should be.

"Mother! Mother!" calls Freckle as she runs indoors. "The strawberries are ripe!"

The other rabbit children jump for joy. They all love strawberries. They go off in a group to Freckle's secret spot, carrying backpacks, bags and baskets. They pick and pick all day long. They pick so many that their bags and baskets are filled to the brim. Luckily, it's a good year for strawberries. There are so many that there are plenty left over for them to eat while picking.

July 3

Too much jam

Mrs. Fluffytail has been in the kitchen all day. It's strawberry season. The children had all gone off to pick strawberries and have come back home with baskets full of them. Unfortunately, strawberries go bad quite quickly. Before you know it, they're covered in mold or else they shrivel up. That's why Mrs. Fluffytail is making jam out of them. "Phew!" she puffs. "This is enough jam to last three years!" She looks at the kitchen table, which is already covered in jars of jam. "Let's tidy this up first!" she decides. She puts a few jars into her basket and takes them into the pantry. She puts the jam jars on a shelf and then fetches some more. After a while, there are two whole shelves filled with jars of jam. "I'm not going to have room for anything else! What shall I do?" she wonders.

July 4

Don't even *mention* jam

"Come on, now, have *another* jam sandwich," says Mrs. Fluffytail, trying to tempt her children. "Oh no! Don't even *mention* jam," moans Harry. "Why do you want us to eat so much of it?" Mother explains: "You all picked so many strawberries that I had to make a hundred jars of jam." "Why did you have to make so many?" asks Harry. "Why?" Mother Rabbit looks a little offended. "I thought it was a terrible waste to let them get moldy."
Harry nods. Yes, that's true. Even so, he still doesn't want any more jam. A hundred jars of it. That means they'll be eating nothing else for a whole year! Something has to be done about it.

July 5   A jam stall

"You've made too much jam, haven't you?" says Harry Fluffytail to his mother.
Mrs. Fluffytail nods.
"Well, I know a way to solve the problem and help us at the same time," beams Harry.
"Tell me how," says his mother.
Harry carefully explains his idea: "I can put a table outdoors to make a stall. Then, I can put all the jam jars in a row on the table, just like in a market. Anyone who wants some jam will have to give me something for it. Not money, but something to eat. Like carrots."
Mrs. Fluffytail thinks it's a very good plan: "You clever boy! Go ahead and do it, but be honest, all right?"

July 6

Jam for sale!

"Jam for sale! Come one, come all!"
Harry calls from his new stall.
"For an apple or a pear,
I've a jar of jam to spare."
At his stall you'll hear him cry
to the curious passerby:
"For a cabbage or a yam,
you can have two jars of jam."
Everything is quickly sold.
Harry's worth his weight in gold.

July 7

Too much energy

"That Leaper of ours just has too much energy," sighs Mrs. Fluffytail. "That child's always doing something. He can't sit still for two seconds!"

"Then we'll have to get him doing something that tires him out," says Father Fluffytail. "Chopping wood perhaps. Then he'd be doing something useful at the same time." "No, it's much too dangerous with that axe," decides his wife. "Shall we make him run around Rabbit Hill three times?"

It makes Father Fluffytail tired just thinking about it. His wife shakes her head: "Leaper has gone around Rabbit Hill at least ten times already today and he doesn't seem the slightest bit tired." Well, then, what are they to do?

July 8

Digging

Mrs. Fluffytail has a long think. She's trying to think of something that will make her son Leaper very tired. Suddenly, she has an idea. Leaper can help her in the vegetable patch. There's lettuce to be planted and carrots to be dug up.

"Come with me to the garden, Leaper!" she calls out. "You're going to help me today."

Soon they're both busy working. Leaper goes to and fro with the heavy wheelbarrow. He hoes and weeds and does his very best. However, Mrs. Fluffytail has to leave for a short while. "I'll be right back," she says to Leaper. "While I'm gone, dig some little holes for planting the lettuces." Digging? Yes! thinks Leaper. He really likes digging!

July 9   Where am I now?

Leaper is helping in the vegetable patch. He's digging a little hole for planting a lettuce. But Leaper! That hole isn't little anymore, it's huge!
Leaper has long ago forgotten why he was digging in the first place. He plows through the earth with his paws. It's going splendidly! He digs deeper and deeper. Soon, he disappears completely underground. But Leaper is so busy digging that he doesn't even notice how dark it's become all around him. After a while, the little rabbit does start to get tired. At long last, he comes back out into the light. He looks all around in great confusion. "Where am I now?" he calls out. "This isn't my mother's vegetable patch!"

July 10   The tunnel

Mr. Longears, the neighbor, is furious. His garden was the most beautiful of all on Rabbit Hill, until Leaper Fluffytail made such a huge hole in it. "Little scamp!" growls Longears. "Just look what you've done! I'll teach you a lesson!"
"B...b...but..." stammers Leaper, "I didn't do it on purpose!"
"That doesn't make any difference!" His neighbor is still angry. "You can fill in the whole tunnel again as punishment. Go on! Get busy!"
Leaper is busy filling in the tunnel for the rest of the day. It's such hard work that by the evening he is completely exhausted. Sleep well, Leaper!

July 11 Are we allowed?

Charlie and Gus Fluffytail want to go exploring together. "Please, Mother, are we allowed?" Mrs. Fluffytail looks at them thoughtfully. Charlie is such a daydreamer and Gus is so terribly clumsy. "Well, I'm not sure...." She hesitates. "We'll be really careful," promise the two brothers. "Oh, all right," says Mrs. Fluffytail, giving way. She has a little plan up her sleeve. As soon as Charlie and Gus have gone, she calls to Tom. Tom Fluffytail is very sensible. That's why she asks him to follow the other two secretly. "That way they'll still think that they're all on their own," she explains to Tom. "And I'll feel a lot happier knowing that you're there if anything happens."

July 12 A rust-colored shadow

Tom Fluffytail creeps through the wood like an Indian brave. Mother Rabbit has asked him to keep an eye on Gus and Charlie. But they mustn't know that he's there. That's why Tom is going on tiptoe a little way behind them. He hides himself behind trees and bushes while Charlie and Gus cheerfully go through the wood. Tom thinks it's a great game. He has to be very careful where he treads. Just one cracking twig and the game is up! Tom is only paying attention to Gus and Charlie, and to his feet, of course. He should be looking around *himself* more! Then he'd notice that he's being followed. A rust-colored shadow has been following Tom's trail for quite a while now. And what might that rust-colored shadow be, do you think?

July 13   Rope

Tom Fluffytail has no idea that Rusty the Fox is following him. He promised his mother to keep an eye on his brothers, Charlie and Gus. And that's why he hasn't been thinking about himself. As soon as Tom realizes that the fox is nearby, he starts to panic. Help! He doubles his speed. But the fox is getting closer and closer. "Oh! I'll never make it!" cries Tom. "He'll catch me for sure!" Suddenly, he sees a rope dangling from a branch. He has no time to think about what the rope is doing there. He grabs one end and climbs up. Once he's reached the branch, he sees two grinning rabbit faces: Charlie and Gus. "We've known for ages you were following us," says Gus. "Mother must've sent you to keep an eye on us," says Charlie. Tom nods. "And now it's the two of you who've saved *me*!"

July 14 **Prettier?**

It's very early in the morning. Mrs. Fluffytail is hopping through the woods with her daughters Roberta and Daisy. They're going to pick herbs so that Mrs. Fluffytail can make medicines from them. And herbs are at their best when picked just before dawn.

Roberta gives a loud yawn and rubs the sleep out of her eyes. She stumbles drowsily after her mother. Luckily it's not cold, even though it's so early. Daisy looks grumpy. She doesn't feel like hopping through the woods at all. She wants to go back to bed. "Silly herbs!" she grumbles. Mrs. Fluffytail turns around.

"Silly herbs?" she asks. "Don't you know how useful they are? You can cure illnesses with some herbs, and others make you look prettier...." Prettier? Daisy suddenly stops looking so grumpy.

July 15 **Herbs**

Rosemary and fresh wild bay,
and peppermint and sage.
All these herbs have been well used
for many a long age.
If you're feeling sick or ill,
then put some in a pan.
Pour on piping hot water
and drink it up you can.
You'll be feeling better fast,
before you've time to say:
"Rosemary and peppermint,
and sage and fresh wild bay."

July 16 Cough medicine

"Why are we picking all these herbs, Mother?" asks Roberta. She's carrying a little basket on her arm that's already filled with rosemary, thyme and many other herbs. Mother Fluffytail explains what she does with the herbs. "I put some herbs in our food. They give the meal an extra-special taste."

"Like parsley in our soup!" remembers Roberta.
"That's right!" says Mrs. Fluffytail. "And I use some herbs for when you are feeling sick. For example, I might make a cough medicine from them."

"Yes, I know," says Daisy shivering. Her mother's cough medicine tastes disgusting. Once you've tasted that, you don't feel like being sick much longer!

July 17 A sensitive plant

Mrs. Fluffytail, Roberta and Daisy have baskets full of herbs. It's time to go back home. "If we hurry, we'll be in time for breakfast with the others!" says Mother.

"Look, Mother!" cries Daisy. "Have you picked that plant there yet?" She stretches out her arm and is about to pick it. But something strange happens. The plant curls all its leaves up tight. "Oh! It doesn't like being touched!" says Daisy, startled.

Mrs. Fluffytail laughs. "Leave that plant alone. It's called a sensitive plant. I'm not going to use that. Just imagine if you were like that. I'd never be able to cuddle you."

135

July 18

Waving good-bye

The next-door neighbor, Mr. Longears, is wearing his shorts and a brightly colored shirt.
He has a pair of sunglasses balanced on his forehead.
"Mr. Fluffytail," he says, "this is the key to our burrow. Would you water our flowers
for us while we're away on vacation?" Father Fluffytail nods. Of course he'll do that for
his neighbor. "Where are you going this year?" he asks.
"We're going to see a distant cousin of mine, Harold Hare. He lives three days away
to the east."
"Gosh, that's a long way," says Father Fluffytail. "You'd better get going."
Mr. Longears agrees. He puts his sunglasses on his nose and sets off with his wife
and seven children.
"See you!" shouts the whole Fluffytail family, waving good-bye.
"Have fun!"

July 19

Three more weeks

"Why is it that we never go on vacation?"
Billy Fluffytail asks his father.
"Would you like to?"
Billy nods. "It sounds wonderful. Discovering all
kinds of new things and making new friends."
"But there are thirteen of us," explains Father
Fluffytail. "Where would the thirteen of us
sleep?"
Billy hadn't thought of that.
"We can't go away just yet anyway," says
Father. "I promised Mr. Longears that I'd keep
an eye on his burrow for the next three weeks.
So that gives you three weeks time to come
up with an idea."

July 20 Summer camp

The Fluffytail family never goes on vacation. "It's much better at home!" says Mr. Fluffytail. But the Fluffytail children don't agree with him. "We want to go on vacation too for once," they complain. That's why Father Fluffytail has come up with a plan. Together with his children, he builds some huts on the grass in front of their rabbit hole. When they're finished, Father Fluffytail says: "You may all sleep here tonight. I'll make a big campfire for roasting carrots. Then it'll seem just like we're far away on vacation." The little Fluffytails are going to have their very own summer camp!

July 21

Double trouble

Twins are quite unusual.
You rarely see a double.
But with the Fluffytails, it seems
that twins are just the trouble!
Hip and Hop you know quite well,
with caps in colors bright.
But Father *also* has a twin.
A most confusing sight!

July 22   **How odd!**

Hip and Hop Fluffytail are playing outdoors. The sun is shining warmly and they're chasing butterflies through the flowers. All at once, they see Father. They go up to him and say: "Hi!"
"Good morning to you, young rabbits!" replies Father.
Hip and Hop look at each other in astonishment. What an odd thing for Father to say! But it doesn't stop there, because they almost fall flat on their backs when Father asks: "Does either of you know where the Fluffytail family's rabbit hole is?" Father must be teasing them. There's no other explanation. So Hip replies and says: "Yes! The same place it was yesterday!" And Hop giggles: "Under the ground!"
But that just makes Father angry. "Impudent monkeys!" he says. "Can't you give a polite answer to a simple question?"
Hip and Hop are quite confused by it all.

July 23   Two fathers?

"Do you think that Father's banged his head?" Hip Fluffytail worriedly
asks his sister Hop. "He's behaving as if he doesn't recognize us.
Perhaps the blow has made him forget everything!"
But his sister doesn't reply. With eyes as big as saucers she points to
something behind him.
Hip turns around and his eyes nearly pop out of his head. He looks to the
left and then he looks to the right. He blinks, and gives his eyes
a good rub. But it doesn't make any difference.
He can see his father when he looks to the left.
But he can also see his father when he looks to the right.
"Two fathers?" he mumbles. "That's impossible.
That means I'll be punished twice every time
I do something naughty."

July 24   Simon

Hip and Hop just don't know what's going on.
They're standing between two rabbits who both
look exactly like their father. Then, one of the
rabbits says to the other: "Simon! Great to see you!"
And the other rabbit replies: "Peter! How are
things?" Hip and Hop let out a sigh of relief.
At least they now know that one of the two rabbits
isn't their father. Their father's name is Peter, not
Simon. "Children, come and meet my twin
brother, Simon," says Father. The other rabbit
starts to laugh. "Now I understand,"
he says. "Your children thought that *I* was their
father." At first, Hip and Hop turn red with
embarrassment. But when they see that Uncle
Simon is laughing, they start laughing too.

July 25   Sailor Simon

Mr. Fluffytail's twin brother is a
sailor. That's why he's often away for
so long. So long, in fact, that the youngest of the Fluffytail
children have never seen him before. Even the oldest children
don't remember him anymore. Only Freckle throws her arms around him
and says : "Hello, Uncle Simon, how are you?" "Fine, little one, fine,"
laughs Simon. "Or I will be when your mother makes me a cup of coffee."
"Coffee?" asks Mrs. Fluffytail, looking confused. Nobody has ever heard of
coffee on Rabbit Hill. The rabbits there drink either fruit juice or milk.
But coffee...what's that?
Simon laughs. "Coffee comes from a faraway, hot country where I
went on my travels," he explains. "I thought it was so good that
I've brought some coffee beans with me. I'll show you how to make
a cup of coffee. A real sailor has to be able to do anything!"

July 26   A great uncle

All eleven of the Fluffytail children are
completely wild about their Uncle Simon now that they
know him better. He plays all kinds of lively games with
them and always knows how to deal with a problem. When
Daisy starts crying after falling down, Uncle Simon takes out a
beautiful handkerchief, which he ties to her knee. The
handkerchief is so pretty that Daisy forgets all about the pain.
And Uncle Simon teaches Gus how to train his ears. After only
a few days, his ears no longer droop quite so badly. "Uncle
Simon's great!" says Harry Fluffytail. And Leaper says: "I reckon
that he's just as brave and clever as Wild Woodsman
Dan."

July 27   Push-ups

"I want to be as big and strong as you when I'm grown up," says Harry to Uncle Simon. "So do we! So do we!" cry his brothers and sisters.
"In that case, you'll have to exercise every day!" laughs Uncle Simon.
"How do you do that?" asks Tom.
"There are lots of ways to do it. Running, skipping, push-ups..." explains Uncle Simon.
"Push-ups?" asks Charlie, not understanding.
Uncle Simon laughs. "You do push-ups on the ground. You lie on your front. Then you put your paws next to your ears and push your body up from the ground. You have to keep your body as straight as a pencil at the same time. Try it." The Fluffytail children try their very best, but doing push-ups isn't easy.

July 28   The test

The Fluffytail children have been exercising very hard all week long. Especially the boys and Roberta, who's just like a boy anyway.
Then, Uncle Simon says: "Today I'm going to see just how hard you've all trained. I'm going to test you!"
"Oh yes! What fun!" The little Fluffytails start dancing about.
"Let's start with..." says Uncle Simon, "who can be first to bring me an apple."
Eleven little Fluffytails dart off at once in all directions. In no time, Uncle Simon is lying happily in the grass, digging into the huge heap of apples that they have brought him. Do you think it was really a test? Or was Uncle Simon just hungry?

July 29 Sailing

"I'd like to go sailing one day," Gus thinks out loud.

Uncle Simon scratches behind his ear. Then he says: "Well, you can."

"How?" asks Gus. He can't believe his ears.

"We'll build a raft together next to the pond. Then, I'll teach you how to sail it."

Gus jumps into the air for joy. Both of them set off for the pond at once. Uncle Simon has brought with him some rope, some nails and a sheet. They'll use tree branches in the woods to make the raft.

"They must be strong branches," says Uncle Simon. By the time their raft is ready, it's nearly dark. "We'll try it out tomorrow," says Gus. "Then I'll really be sailing."

July 30   Fresh water

The raft is bobbing up and down on the pond. Gus is as proud as can be. He built it himself, together with Uncle Simon. It has a real sail and a rudder to steer with. Gus is to be the captain, says Uncle Simon. "Cast off the ropes, sailor!" Gus calls out to his uncle, and they slowly sail away.

With his tongue hanging out of his mouth, Gus steers the raft across the pond. He has to keep his attention fixed on the rudder, so he doesn't notice Uncle Simon. After a while, Gus feels a bit safer and says: "This is great isn't it, Uncle Simon?" But Uncle Simon doesn't reply. Uncle Simon has turned a green color. Uncle Simon is seasick. "But Uncle, I thought you never felt seasick!" The sailor replies weakly: "Not on the sea, but that is salt water. This pond is full of sweet, fresh water and I can't handle it."

July 31
Sweet water sick

The more waves,
the more pleasure.
A real brave sailor
just sees it as leisure.
A real brave sailor
does not mind one bit.
As long as the water
is salty, he's fit.
But if it should be that
the water is sweet,
the bravest of sailors
feels sick to his feet.
And grasshopper green, he
will cry to his mate
to let out the anchor
before it's too late.

143

August 1   Girls' chores

The sun rises very early in summer. It's already hot outside when the Fluffytail children come out of their rabbit hole in the morning. "Phew!" puffs Roberta. "I'm going back indoors. At least it's nice and cool inside our burrow."
But as soon as she enters the kitchen she sees that Mother Fluffytail is ready to start doing all kinds of chores. There's always something to do: sweeping, doing the dishes and cleaning. Roberta hates those sorts of chores. Silly girls' chores, she thinks. She makes an excuse and disappears outside again. Mrs. Fluffytail knows very well that Roberta doesn't want to help her in the kitchen. But Mrs. Fluffytail also knows that everyone has to help with the household chores once in a while. Even little tomboy rabbits like Roberta.

August 2

Watering

"Roberta!" calls Mrs. Fluffytail. "Come back here." Oh! Oh! thinks Roberta, now I'm going to get it! Her mother comes out of the rabbit hole and waits until Roberta has come up to her. Then she says:
"I think you could help me for once." "Yes, but..." begins Roberta. "I don't want any excuses," says Mrs. Fluffytail sharply. "I want you to give the flowers some water." That changes everything. All at once, Roberta starts thinking what fun helping out can be. Watering the flowers! That means she can play with lots of water! She starts filling up the watering can right away. It keeps her busy all morning. With a happy smile, Roberta finally puts away the watering can and Mrs. Fluffytail strokes her ears. "There you are," she says. "Not all girls' chores are so boring, are they?"

3 August

An Indian brave

In a distant mountain land of
shining lakes and forests vast,
lived an Indian brave of legend,
creature from a dim and distant past.

Striped with red his face was painted.
He wore feathers in his hair.
Buffalo and deer he hunted.
His best friend the great brown bear.

4 August

Indian rabbits

"Go on, Uncle Simon, tell us about your
adventures," beg the little Fluffytails time and
again. They just adore their uncle's stories.
They listen as quiet as mice when he tells them
about his adventures in far-off places. Uncle Simon
scratches his head. "Have I told you about the Indian
rabbits yet?" he asks. "Indian rabbits?
No, what are they?" asks Harry. "They live far from
here. Where the land is covered by great lakes and
mountains and forests as far as you can see.
The Indian rabbits are different from us.
They live in tents called wigwams and wear
feathers on their heads."
"Why do they do that?" asks Harry
curiously.
"Because it looks pretty, I *think*,"
replies Uncle Simon.

August 5
Bow and arrow

Uncle Simon is telling the children a story about Indian rabbits. They live in wigwams and hunt with bows and arrows. Harry wrinkles his nose. Those Indian rabbits seem very strange to him. Why would they wear feathers on their heads? However, the bow and arrow part sounds more interesting. Harry slips quietly away while Uncle Simon is still talking to the others. He wants to make his own bow. He takes a piece of elastic from his mother's sewing basket. After a lot of searching he finds a bent piece of branch. All I need now, he thinks, are just a few straight twigs to use as arrows. Then I can start shooting them into the air.

August 6   **Feathers**

Harry Fluffytail has made a bow and some arrows from a branch and twigs. He's practicing with them, but it isn't going very well. "Hey, Harry, what are you doing?" comes a voice behind him. It's Uncle Simon. "I...er...I'm practicing being an Indian." "But don't you know that you need feathers to do that?" asks Uncle Simon. "I'm not putting feathers on *my* head!" protests Harry. Uncle Simon chuckles: "They're not for your head. Real Indian rabbits put feathers at the end of their arrows. That makes the arrows fly better through the air. Wait a moment, let me help you." Phew, thinks Harry, at least I don't have to wear any feathers.

August 7

Farewell!

Farewell! You're off to sea.
I'll wave you from the quay.
Why can it not be me?
Alas, that's not to be.
Farewell! You're off to sea.

August 8 Oh, please stay!

"Why must you go so soon?" asks Freckle. She isn't at
all happy that Uncle Simon is going to leave them yet
again. "Oh, please stay!" she says. "You can sleep in my
bed and there's enough to eat. I'll look after you."
Uncle Simon smiles. "That's very kind of you,
Freckle," he says, "but I think I should tell you
something. The reason I became a sailor is because
I can't stay long in the same place. I soon start
getting the itch to move on again, however
kind you all are to me."
Freckle bravely holds back her tears and tries
hard to understand. Uncle Simon strokes her
ears. "I promise to come back soon," he says.
"And you never know. When I do, I might
just bring you back something from a
faraway country."

August 9   **Seeing Uncle off**

The Fluffytail children are all feeling a little sad. Their Uncle Simon is leaving them today. He's going off to sea again.

Come on, children," says Father Fluffytail at breakfast. "I have a surprise for you all if you only cheer up a little bit." A surprise! Right away, the little Fluffytails forget all about feeling sad. "What is it, Father? Go on, tell us!" Father Fluffytail clears his throat and says with a serious look: "We're all going to take Uncle Simon to his ship to see him off. It'll be a day out for us. A day at the seaside!" Hooray! That *is* a nice surprise.

August 10   **The ship**

The Fluffytail children are having such fun! Along with their parents, they're taking their Uncle Simon to his ship. There were all kinds of things to see in the harbor. So many ships, so many flags!

Uncle Simon even let them come on board. They saw the ship's little kitchen, which sailors call a galley. They also saw Uncle Simon's cabin. "What a small bed you have!" cries Tom Fluffytail. "Don't you fall out of it with all the big waves?"

Uncle Simon just laughs. "No, I don't. I rock to and fro with the waves. They send me straight to sleep."

At the end of the afternoon, the ship sets sail. The Fluffytails stand on the quay for ages waving farewell.

Good-bye, Uncle Simon, come back soon!

August 11   Dull

"It's so dull without Uncle Simon," sighs Leaper Fluffytail. His brothers and sisters all agree with him. They had the most wonderful time with their uncle. He always came up with fun new games to play. Or else he would tell them the most exciting stories. Almost more exciting than the stories about Wild Woodsman Dan. Now that Uncle Simon has gone, the little Fluffytails have to think of things to do by themselves. And that isn't so easy. They just sit around and sigh a lot to themselves. All at once, they hear someone clearing his throat behind them. It's Father Fluffytail. "So, girls and boys," he says, "you wouldn't all be sitting around with nothing to do, would you?" What is he holding behind his back?

August 12

Kites

"Your Uncle Simon left something behind for you all," says Father Fluffytail. From behind his back, he produces colorful, diamond-shaped pieces of paper with strings of ribbons attached. Eleven little rabbit mouths all gasp at once. "Kites!" Father nods. "And today, I'm going to teach you how to fly them." They all go off to an open space, because you need space to be able to fly a kite. First, they all choose a kite. There's a yellow kite with the sun's face on it, a blue kite with a seagull, a green one with a dragon and lots more besides. It's so difficult to choose.

August 13   **A wonderful sight**

The little Fluffytails are standing neatly in a line.
They've all been given a kite from their Uncle
Simon. Now, they have to learn how to fly them.
Father Rabbit is going to help.
Gus is the first to try. He's chosen a purple kite with
a bat on it.
"Hold the string tightly," explains Father.
"Then run with the kite to the far side of
the field and hold it up high. Pull on
the string as soon as the wind catches
the kite." Gus nods. After a few tries, it
works. Gosh! Look how high the kite
flies. Then the second little rabbit has a
turn. And then the third, and so on.
Once all eleven kites are in the air, Father
Fluffytail has to take a rest.
He's quite exhausted from all that helping.
But then he looks up and sees all the pretty
kites high in the sky. It's such a wonderful
sight that he completely forgets
how tired he is.

August 14 Sheep

"Let's get busy!" says Mrs. Fluffytail, clapping her hands.
"Today we're going off to where the sheep are grazing."
They're going to collect some wool. There's a whole lot of
wool stuck on the barbed wire fence that surrounds
Farmer Smith's sheep field. The wool gets stuck on the
barbed wire whenever the sheep walk past the fence.
If they all work hard, they can collect quite a lot of
wool in just one afternoon. Enough to make new
sweaters for the whole family.

August 15 Far too many

The Fluffytails walk one behind the other toward
the sheep field where they're going to gather wool.
Billy is dawdling behind. "Come on, Billy, hurry up!"
calls Father Fluffytail. But only a little while later, Billy is
once more a long way behind them all. He joins the others at
the field a whole quarter of an hour later. Father Fluffytail
gives him a scolding. "It's much too hot to collect wool," moans
Billy. Mother Fluffytail shakes her head. "But Billy," she
explains, "you're all growing so fast that you need two new
sweaters each. And I have to knit them all before
winter comes!" That's true. Billy tries to work out
how many sweaters his mother will have to knit:
one, two, three... Phew, far too many, he
decides.

August 16 Run for it!

The Fluffytails are all collecting wool, their faces flushed from the heat. They're picking wool off the barbed wire fence. It's hot and tiring work. Picking, hopping on a little way, picking some more, and so on. Billy Fluffytail is getting tired of it. Suddenly, he has an idea. Farmer Smith's sheep are grazing just a little way off. Billy slowly creeps toward them. He chooses the sheep with the thickest wool and...pulls on its fleece. Baaa! Baaa! The sheep is very startled and it starts to chase after Billy. Billy runs for his life. No, it wasn't such a good idea after all. Luckily, the sheep is feeling very hot as well, much too hot to run far. It looks at Billy angrily. What a naughty rabbit!

153

August 17   **Swimming**

It really is extremely hot today. Father Fluffytail looks at
the thermometer. It points to more than eighty-five degrees!
"This is no weather for working," he decides. "It's the sort
of weather for swimming."
So, out come all the swimsuits, and Mother Fluffytail
quickly grabs a whole heap of towels.
Then, the entire family sets off for the pond.
They find a nice spot among the tall reeds
and rushes.
"This is where we'll put our beach towels,"
says Father. But the children all dive into
the water right away without
listening. Mmm! How
beautifully cool it is!

August 18

Swimming lesson

Breaststroke, crawl or butterfly,
but learn to swim you must.
Water in your nose or not,
keep trying till you bust!

August 19

All heads under

Gosh! I'll bet
It's really wet!
That's no wonder!
All heads under!

Splutter, splatter...
My teeth chatter.
Let's go swim
and jump right in!

August 20

Not so bad

Daisy Fluffytail is
standing at the
edge of the pond.
She's been
paddling in the
shallow water, but
that's as far as she'll go.
If she goes any farther
into the water, her pretty
pink swimsuit will get wet.
Let the others splash about. She
turns around to walk back to her
towel. Watch out, Daisy! Harry's
behind you with a bucket of water. One,
two, three...splash! Harry's emptied his
bucket...all over Daisy! Now she's
completely soaking. "Nasty boy!" shouts
Daisy angrily. She chases after her brother,
running smack into the water.
Harry's far out of reach, of course.
In any case, Daisy decides that
the water isn't so bad after all.

155

August 21 Fairyland

Tom Fluffytail awakes with a start. He's just had a bad dream. So he gets out of bed to have a drink of water.
But as Tom goes into the hall, he forgets all about how thirsty he was. He sees a bright light streaming underneath the front door.
"What can that be?" Tom wonders. "Has the sun come up in the middle of the night?"
Curiously, he opens the door. Then, he understands. It's nearly full moon. The moonbeams cast a strange light all over the Wild Wood. It's nighttime and yet still a little like daytime. It looks like a picture out of fairyland.

August 22 Full moon

Tom Fluffytail can't stop talking at breakfast.
"Tonight, there's going to be a full moon. That only happens once a month. And...and..." He nearly chokes from all the excitement. What is it that's getting Tom so excited? It's because Tom knows what's going to happen. Every year in August, the rabbits of Rabbit Hill celebrate with a summer moon party. They all gather together under the light of the full moon. They make a big campfire and sing songs.

156

August 23   **Party**

A great bonfire is burning on the top of Rabbit Hill. The flames are licking up high into the sky and the moon is full. The moon's beams light up the whole hill. In its gentle light, the rabbits are dancing around and around the campfire. It's their summer moon party. There's a story that is told about it. That story is very, very old, and nobody knows who first told it. The story goes that any rabbit who dances a hundred times around the campfire under the light of the summer full moon will become as brave and fearless as Wild Woodsman Dan. Some rabbits don't believe the story, and anyway, they're all enjoying themselves so much that they soon lose count. But many rabbits believe that the story is true. And not only them. Even Rusty the Fox believes it. He skulks behind a tree in the shadows and watches the party, not daring to come any closer.

August 24

Moody morning

My goodness! Don't the twins look grumpy! Hip and Hop
went to bed much too late the night before. They stayed up right
until the end of the summer moon party. And once they were
tucked in bed, they kept on chatting for a long time.
It's fun to be allowed to stay up so late, of course, but the next
morning Hip couldn't get out of bed and Hop fell asleep
at breakfast.
While their brothers and sisters play happily together
outside, Hip and Hop are dozing under a tree. All that
racket! No, they're not ready for that at the moment.
Hip even grumbles about the blackbird that is singing
such a pretty song above him in the tree.
"My! My!" scolds the blackbird. "How moody you
are this morning!"

August 25   Noise and light

"What is the matter with Hip and Hop?" Father
Fluffytail asks his wife. "Oh, those two haven't had
enough sleep," she explains. "Well, they'll just have
to catch up on their sleep," decides Father. He
sends the twins straight back to bed.
So there Hip and Hop lie. All tucked in. But
however tired they are, they just can't get to
sleep. "I can't get to sleep with all the noise,"
complains Hip. "And there's so much light
coming through the curtains," sighs Hop. That
gives Hip an idea. "Come on, Hop," he says.
"Take the pillows off all the beds." Hop looks at
him curiously, but she does as he says. What is
Hip going to do with all those pillows?

158

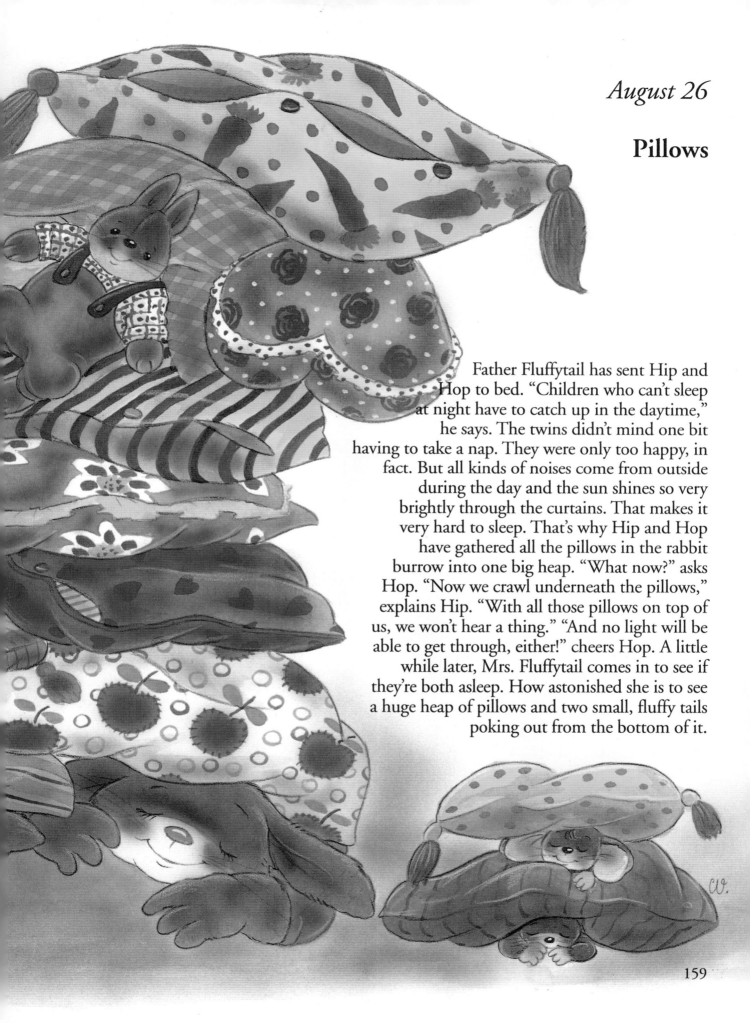

Pillows

Father Fluffytail has sent Hip and Hop to bed. "Children who can't sleep at night have to catch up in the daytime," he says. The twins didn't mind one bit having to take a nap. They were only too happy, in fact. But all kinds of noises come from outside during the day and the sun shines so very brightly through the curtains. That makes it very hard to sleep. That's why Hip and Hop have gathered all the pillows in the rabbit burrow into one big heap. "What now?" asks Hop. "Now we crawl underneath the pillows," explains Hip. "With all those pillows on top of us, we won't hear a thing." "And no light will be able to get through, either!" cheers Hop. A little while later, Mrs. Fluffytail comes in to see if they're both asleep. How astonished she is to see a huge heap of pillows and two small, fluffy tails poking out from the bottom of it.

August 27

Thorns

Hidden well among its leaves,
begging to be picked,
hang its berries black and ripe,
but do not be tricked!
Beware the bramble's weapon sharp.
The spine and thorn that catches.
Or else, instead of berries sweet,
you'll only end with scratches.

August 28

Blackberries

Charlie and Tom
love blackberries. The
only thing is that it's so
difficult
to pick them because
of all the thorns. But Tom
is clever: he digs a tunnel
under all the brambles so
they can eat blackberries
from the bush
whenever they want.

August 29   **Hungry**

Rusty the Fox is creeping around the blackberry bush. Rusty doesn't like blackberries. He only eats them if he's really hungry, like today. He's just about to sink his teeth into a juicy blackberry when he smells something. Rabbit! He immediately forgets all about the blackberry. He looks to see where the scent is coming from and finds Tom and Charlie Fluffytail, who are playing together. Rusty's tummy begins to rumble just looking at the tasty twosome. Tom and Charlie are terrified. Help! Rusty Fox! "Quickly, Charlie!" Tom grabs his brother by the collar and drags him to the tunnel that he's dug. It takes them to safety in the middle of the brambles. "Rusty can't get us here!" says Tom. "And we can stay here for ages," says Charlie, pointing at all the blackberries. "There's lots to eat!"

August 30

Mail

"Rat-a-tat-tat!" goes Dickie the Carrier Pigeon as he taps his beak against the door. Mr. Fluffytail opens it.
"Oh, hello, Dickie. Do you have any letters for us?"
Dickie nods. He takes a postcard out of his sack.
Mr. Fluffytail starts to laugh.
"Children!" he calls cheerfully. "There's a postcard from Uncle Simon. He's in Africa now. He misses us a bit. He may come back to see us at Christmas."
The Fluffytails each look at the postcard in turn.
It shows a picture of a golden beach and coconut palm trees.
It's such fun getting mail!

August 31

Letters

I'm writing you a letter so
that I can be quite sure you know
that I have not forgotten you
and that I'm thinking of you too.
And has my letter made you glad?
Remember me when you feel sad.
Pick up a pen and then write me
as long a letter as can be.

163

September 1 Sick?

"What is the matter with Billy?" asks Mother Fluffytail with concern. Her son doesn't look well. He has dark circles under his eyes and has been feeling drowsy for days. "You're to take a nap this afternoon!" says Father Fluffytail firmly. Billy nods, and after lunch he dutifully goes off to bed.

Mother and Father Rabbit can't understand it. It's beautiful weather outside. Usually they find it difficult to get their children to bed at this time of year. No, there's definitely something the matter with Billy. But what? "I hope he's not getting sick," worries Mother.

September 2 Nightingale

Billy isn't sick. Not at all. He's just tired. And do you know why? Every night, while everyone's asleep, Billy gets out of bed and quietly creeps outside, where he sits underneath the great oak tree. Every night, a little bird perches on a branch high up in the oak tree. It's a small, dark-colored bird, nothing very special at first glance. But once the bird starts to sing, it sounds so beautiful that it gives you goose bumps. The bird is called a nightingale.

"Oh, if only I could sing as beautifully as that!" sighs Billy as he creeps back into bed again. Exhausted, he falls asleep at once and dreams that he can sing just as beautifully as the little bird. And that he's allowed to take an afternoon nap every day.

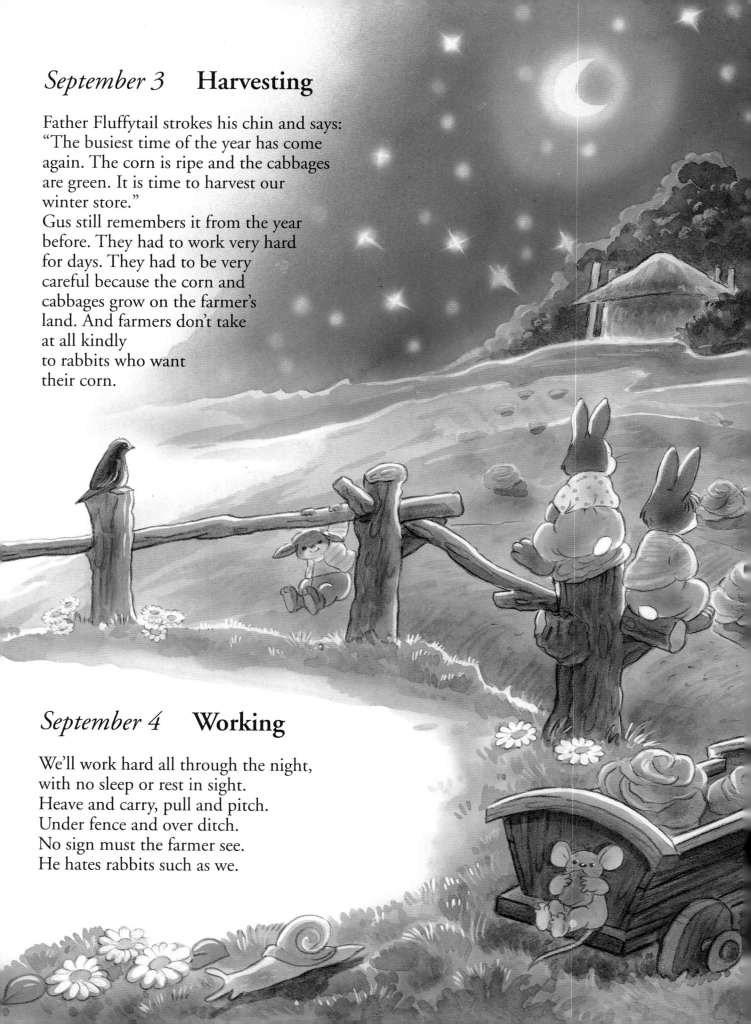

September 3   Harvesting

Father Fluffytail strokes his chin and says:
"The busiest time of the year has come
again. The corn is ripe and the cabbages
are green. It is time to harvest our
winter store."
Gus still remembers it from the year
before. They had to work very hard
for days. They had to be very
careful because the corn and
cabbages grow on the farmer's
land. And farmers don't take
at all kindly
to rabbits who want
their corn.

September 4   Working

We'll work hard all through the night,
with no sleep or rest in sight.
Heave and carry, pull and pitch.
Under fence and over ditch.
No sign must the farmer see.
He hates rabbits such as we.

September 5   List

Mr. Fluffytail has made a list. First, the cart needs fixing. They need the cart to bring the corn and cabbages back to their burrow. "Tom and Gus can do that!" he decides. "The girls can help Mother make a flask of lemonade and some sandwiches. It's going to be hard work tonight so you're all going to feel hungry." "But..." asks Gus, confused, "won't there be plenty of cabbages for us to eat in the fields?" "Yes!" laughs his father. "But we're going to save the cabbages for the winter. You're forbidden to eat any of them tonight. Otherwise, you'll be eating until you're sick."

September 6   A nice job

Night has fallen. The farmers are in their homes. The Fluffytail family quietly creeps toward the cabbage field. They stand quite still at its edge. "Billy and Leaper have the best eyes," says Father. "They will keep watch. Watch out especially for the farmer's cat. He's extremely nasty." While the others are busy picking cabbages, Leaper says: "Isn't this a nice job? The others have much harder work to do." Just then, they hear something in the bushes. Leaper jumps out of his skin. Luckily, it was only a bird!

September 7

Far too full

Once they have gathered together a great heap of cabbages, Father says: "That's enough. Time to go back home. Just put the cabbages on the cart!" But, oh dear! They have far too many cabbages. They won't all fit on the cart. What will they do? "It's a shame to leave them here," says Mother.

September 8

How heavy it is!

What are the Fluffytails going to do now? They can't get all the cabbages onto the cart. Everyone thinks it's a real pity to leave the rest behind.
"Then we'll just have to carry them," decides Father Fluffytail. "The girls can help Mother to pull along the cart, while each one of us strong men carries back a cabbage." Roberta starts complaining right away: "I'm strong too! I want to carry a cabbage! As if girls can't do that!" But she's soon sorry. The cabbage is much too big and heavy for her little rabbit paws. Her brothers are panting and groaning under the weight as well, and Gus keeps dropping his cabbage. No, this idea isn't going to work.

September 9   **Clever Tom**

Father Rabbit, Roberta, Leaper, Billy, Gus, Charlie, Hip and Harry all sigh at once. Each one of them is carrying a heavy cabbage in their arms. The only one not to make a sound is Tom. Clever Tom has thought of something better. He's not carrying his cabbage. No, he's rolling his in front of him. That makes it a lot easier. The others also try Tom's method. "Yippee! This is great!" shouts Harry. "Good idea, Tom!" Before they know it, they're home...and with all the cabbages too!

September 10

More work still

Mrs. Fluffytail is standing contentedly in the pantry. The cabbage shelf is completely full.
"Now, whatever happens, we'll have enough vitamins to last all winter," she sighs happily.
Then, she picks out a nice, green cabbage. She's going to use it to make a soup. She knows that her children love cabbage soup. Tonight, they'll have a feast. And that's just as well, because there is more work still to be done. The corn is ripe. Before the farmers start using their great machines to pick all the corn, the rabbits must also bring in their own corn harvest.

September 11

Cabbage soup

Hear me cry, and howl and whoop.
Fill my bowl with cabbage soup!
I could do a loop-the-loop
when I've had my cabbage soup.
Can't you see I'm cock-a-hoop?
Give me more hot cabbage soup!

170

September 12   **What a mess!**

"Do we really have to go to work again?" whines Charlie. Of all the Fluffytail children, he finds it the hardest. Charlie loves sleeping. And now he must stay up late again. Tonight, they're all going off to pick corn. Father and Mother Fluffytail know just how hard it is on Charlie. "Do you know what?" says Father. "You can stay at home." Charlie can't believe his ears. He doesn't have to work! But then, Father says: "We can be off right away if you do the dishes and the cleaning up." Charlie looks silently at the pile of plates and dirty pans. What a mess! "I think I'll go with you after all," he says quietly.

September 13

I'm not scared

The corn rustles softly as the Fluffytail family busily picks the corncobs. Now and then they hear a twig break. Then they take a big, ripe corncob and, holding it in their paws, they wait in silence. The farmer's big, ginger tomcat might be prowling around nearby. "Aren't you scared?" Charlie whispers to Harry. "Me? Scared of that fat old cat? No way!" boasts Harry. Charlie sighs and quietly goes on with picking corn. Suddenly, his nose starts to itch. "Ah...ah...tchoo!" he sneezes. Brave Harry is so scared by the noise that he climbs up to the top of a corn plant. "Don't ever do that again!" comes his trembling little voice from up above.

September 14   Secret hideaway

"Hop!" calls Hip. "Are you coming? Let's go to our secret place!"
he says. The twins really do have a secret place.
They've made a hideaway inside a hollow in the ground.
First, they made it deeper. Next, they covered it in branches
and twigs. And last, they covered the roof with grass.
You'd never guess it was there unless you'd been
shown it first.

September 15

Matches

Hip and Hop are sitting in their secret
hideaway. "Why did you ask me to come
here?" asks Hop. Hip doesn't reply.
He searches in his pocket with a serious
look on his face and takes out a little box.
"What's that?" asks Hop. But then she sees
what it is: a box of matches.
"Oh, Hip!" she cries out. "Mother and
Father said that matches aren't allowed!"
"Shh! Quiet!" warns Hip. This is Uncle
Simon's matchbox. He left it behind
when he went away. "I just want to see
for myself if matches really are so
dangerous."

September 16   A fight

The twins are having a fight for the first time in their lives. Hop shouts crossly: "We're not allowed to play with matches. I'm not doing it! You're really stupid!" And Hip shouts back: "If you're too scared, then just go away!" Hop decides to tell Mother Fluffytail. "Matches? The naughty rabbit! That's just how accidents start!"

September 17   Angry

Father Fluffytail is really very angry indeed. Hip has some matches and is playing with them. Hop shows Father where the secret hideaway is. Even at a distance, they see smoke coming from the hideaway's roof. Father runs quickly ahead and pulls Hip, coughing and choking, out of the hollow Hip won't ever play with fire again!

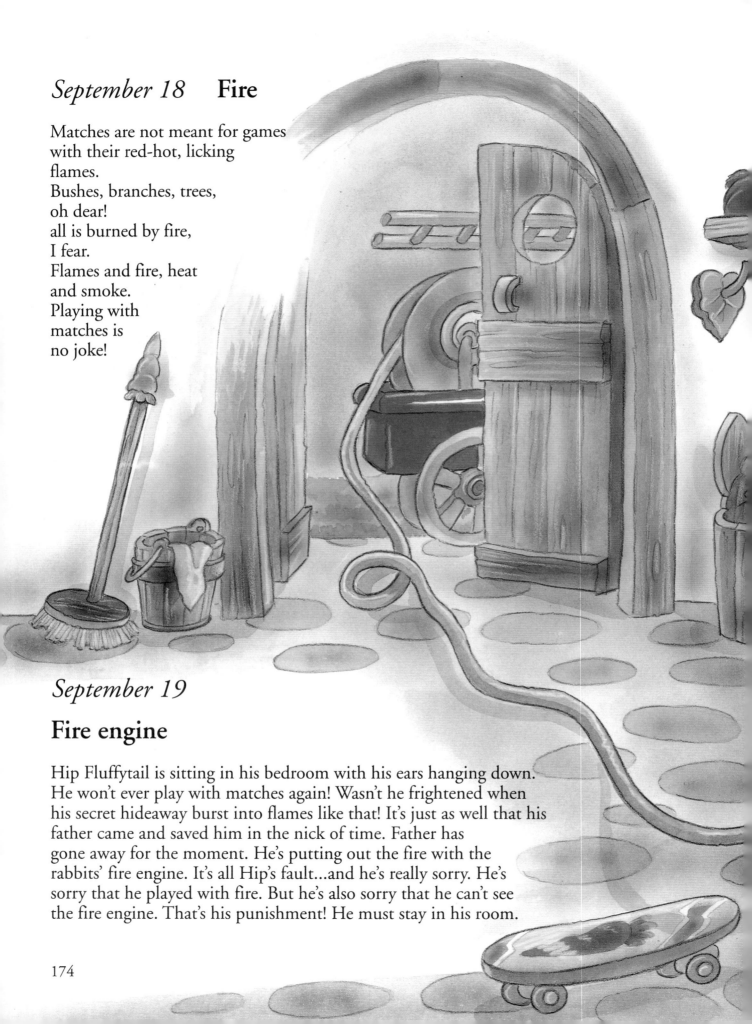

September 18   Fire

Matches are not meant for games
with their red-hot, licking
flames.
Bushes, branches, trees,
oh dear!
all is burned by fire,
I fear.
Flames and fire, heat
and smoke.
Playing with
matches is
no joke!

September 19

Fire engine

Hip Fluffytail is sitting in his bedroom with his ears hanging down.
He won't ever play with matches again! Wasn't he frightened when
his secret hideaway burst into flames like that! It's just as well that his
father came and saved him in the nick of time. Father has
gone away for the moment. He's putting out the fire with the
rabbits' fire engine. It's all Hip's fault...and he's really sorry. He's
sorry that he played with fire. But he's also sorry that he can't see
the fire engine. That's his punishment! He must stay in his room.

174

September 20   Punishment

"So, young rabbit!" says Father Fluffytail to Hip. Father is still wearing his firefighters' uniform. He has just put out the fire that Hip started. "Yes, Father?" mumbles Hip nervously. He's expecting to be punished.

"Now do you understand how dangerous fire can be?" asks Father.

"Yes, Father. I'll never do it again," promises Hip.

"Hmmm." Father Rabbit can see how very sorry Hip is. Even so, he still thinks that Hip should be taught a lesson.

"The fire engine is covered from top to bottom in soot. As punishment, you're to clean it all off now," he says. "And once you've finished, I want you to write out one hundred times: 'Children may not play with fire because it is much too dangerous.'"

"Yes, Father," replies Hip. He'll do anything, as long as Father stops being so mad at him.

175

September 21   **Fluffy tail**

Daisy Fluffytail is sitting with her fluffy tail in the
sun. She's very proud of her silky little tail.
She washes it in cold water every day and brushes
it for hours. "Nobody has a tail as nice as mine. Who
wouldn't want to swap tails with me?" she sings gleefully.
"Caw! Caw!" comes a sound from above. It's Casey the Crow.
He looks at her boldly with his narrow, black eyes. "What did you
say, Daisy?" he croaks. "Swap tails with you?
I don't think so!" Then he flies away and Daisy is left alone.
What can Casey have meant?

September 22

Silky tail

Hear small Daisy sing and laugh:
"Mine's the softest tail by half,
and, what's more, the purest white.
What a splendid, charming sight!
Whose face wouldn't beam and shine
with a silky tail like mine?"

September 23   The prettiest

"Silly crow," mumbles Daisy. "I'll bet he'd love to have a pretty little tail like mine really."
But the crow *has* made Daisy wonder. She decides to go and ask the other animals who has the prettiest tail. "Hazel!" she calls out to the squirrel. "Who has the prettiest tail?" "I have, of course!" says Hazel. "Look how bushy and red it is!" Then she asks the deer. "Why, our tails are prettiest, of course," reply the deer. "Underneath they're a beautiful white so our children can see us in the twilight."
Daisy keeps going. Nobody thinks that her tail is the prettiest.

September 24

A funny thought

Daisy has a problem. None of the animals in the wood thinks that her tail is pretty. Father Rabbit can't help himself from laughing at his vain daughter. "All animals have the tails that suit them," he explains to her. "A fluffy tail suits a rabbit. But can you imagine a crow with a little fluffy tail on its behind?" No, Daisy can't imagine that. The very thought is so funny it makes her laugh. Casey the Crow would look so odd!

September 25   Visitor

"Knock! Knock!" Someone's knocking on the
Fluffytail family's door. Father Rabbit goes to open it.
It's Willy Whitewhiskers. Willy is a big boy rabbit.
He also lives on Rabbit Hill, but on the other side.
Willy has been visiting them quite a lot just recently.
Harry and Leaper Fluffytail begin to giggle.
"I'll bet he's in love with Freckle!" they whisper
But Freckle overhears them. "That's not true!"
she says. But she turns such a bright red that
you can't see her freckles anymore.

September 26

Strolling

Willy Whitewhiskers has come to ask Freckle if she
wants to go for a stroll with him. Mrs. Fluffytail looks
at her daughter. Freckle looks at her so sweetly. She
obviously wants to go for a stroll very much. "All
right," says Mother. "But only if Harry goes too, and
you have to be back in an hour." "And Willy must
keep an eye out for Rusty the Fox!" warns Father.
Of course he will. Willy is a distant relation to
Wild Woodsman Dan!

September 27

Gosh!

Harry Fluffytail is bored. Mother told him to go along with Willy and Freckle. But those two are so dull! They don't say anything. They just hold paws and sigh to each other as they stroll through the wood. Harry walks off in a bad mood. Let them sigh all they like. He's going off on an adventure. But after only a few steps he hears something rustling. He turns around and... he's standing face to face with Rusty the Fox. "Help!" Luckily, Willy hears him. He chases the fox away with a few well-aimed pebbles. Harry is safe! "Thank you, Willy!" says Harry gratefully.

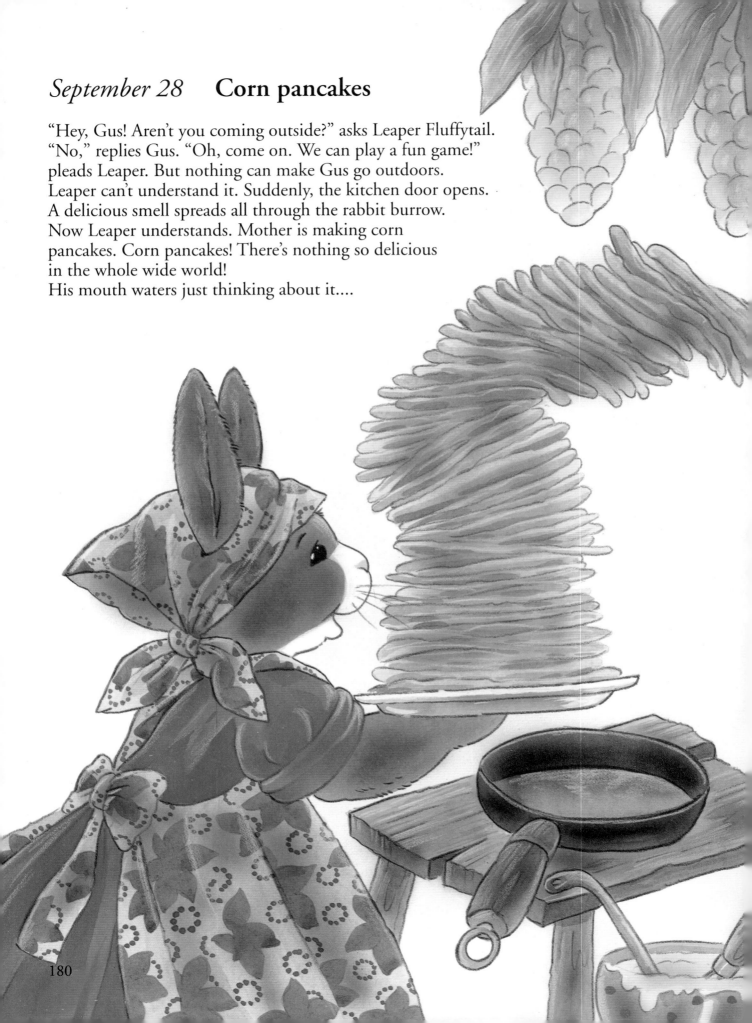

September 28   **Corn pancakes**

"Hey, Gus! Aren't you coming outside?" asks Leaper Fluffytail.
"No," replies Gus. "Oh, come on. We can play a fun game!"
pleads Leaper. But nothing can make Gus go outdoors.
Leaper can't understand it. Suddenly, the kitchen door opens.
A delicious smell spreads all through the rabbit burrow.
Now Leaper understands. Mother is making corn
pancakes. Corn pancakes! There's nothing so delicious
in the whole wide world!
His mouth waters just thinking about it....

September 29   Waiting in line

Gus and Leaper are standing next to the kitchen door. "What are you two doing there?" ask Hip and Hop. Gus and Leaper are sniffing the air, rubbing their tummies and licking their lips.

Hip and Hop understand at once: Mother is making corn pancakes. They go and stand behind their brothers. A little later, Billy and Charlie appear. Then, Roberta, Daisy, Freckle, Harry and Tom. At last, the kitchen door opens. "Children! Come and sit at the ta...!" Mother starts to say. But then she sees all her children waiting there in a line, and she bursts out laughing. Those clever little rabbits. They always know when they're going to get corn pancakes.

September 30

Tasty!

Take some corncobs, golden bright.
Grind them into flour light.
With an egg and milk, be brisk.
Put them in a bowl and whisk.
When you've followed all these tips,
quickly fry and lick your lips.

181

October 1 Very old

Tom Fluffytail is sitting on a high ridge. He's given his glasses an extra polish today. He wants to be able to see everything, because his grandparents are coming to stay. Grandpa is always jolly and tells wonderful stories. And Grandma is the kindest grandma in the whole world. But Grandpa and Grandma are very old. Tom knows that they're going to feel very tired from their long journey. That's why he's gone ahead to meet them and help carry their heavy suitcases the last part of the way. "Where are they?" sighs Tom. His eyes start to ache from staring into the distance. Worried, he looks along the path again. There's nothing to be seen. Only a flock of geese high above him, flying through the sky. And it's getting dark!

October 2

Flying

A great gray goose descends out of the sky. Tom looks up in wonder. The goose lands and two rabbits climb off its back. It's Grandpa and Grandma! Grandpa laughs. "Hello, young fellow! We didn't feel like hopping all the way. That's why we flew!"

October 3 A little scared

What fun it is in the Fluffytail's rabbit burrow! There are fifteen of them now, counting Grandpa and Grandma. That sounds like a lot of confusion, but when Grandpa and Grandma are there, the little Fluffytails behave themselves perfectly. Freckle brings in a cup of tea. "Thank you, my dear!" says Grandma. "That's just what I need after my long flight." Grandma and Grandpa flew on the back of a gray goose, and Grandma was a little scared. "I'm glad to be on the ground again with my own two feet," she says.

October 4 Imagination

Grandpa Fluffytail had a lot of adventures in the past. When he was a young rabbit, he even knew Wild Woodsman Dan. He often tells his grandchildren about the rabbit hero. Just listen to the stories he tells: "So, Charlie, Woodsman Dan and I both chased away the Crow Hunters. He sat on a great horned owl, and I flew on my faithful snowy owl...." "Hmm!" says Grandma, clearing her throat. "I imagine you were *just* as scared as me up there in the sky."

October 5   Wild Grandpa

When Grandpa, in his younger days,
through hills and dales ran,
they were a pair of cutups,
both he and Woodsman Dan.
"There's nothing that we didn't dare.
How brave we were. How bold.
And with all rascals we dealt fair.
But now I'm stiff and old."

October 6   Walking stick

"That's enough chatter for now!" says Grandpa.
"I'm going to take a little stroll." But try as he might, he
can't get out of his chair. Grandpa looks around.
He's looking for his stick. It's fallen down next to his chair.
Charlie gets it for him. It's a very nice walking stick. It has
little carved figures on it that have been colored in. "There
you are, Grandpa," says Charlie. "Now you can stand up
again." "Humph!" splutters Grandpa. "I can stand up
perfectly well without a stick. I just need
it for dealing with any rascals I find." Charlie
looks at Grandpa. Is he serious? How is it he
couldn't get out of his chair, then?"

185

October 7   On the warpath

Perhaps you've heard of spring cleaning. In spring, human beings often get the feeling that the whole house must be cleaned from top to bottom. Rabbits also get the same feeling, but in the autumn. Every bit of dust and dirt has to be cleaned out of the rabbit burrow. "Watch out, children!" laughs Father Fluffytail. "Your mother's on the warpath again." "Warpath?" says Gus with alarm. War means fighting, and Gus doesn't like fighting at all. Father strokes his ears: "It's all right! The only fight your mother's having is one against all the dust and dirt. Just look, she's already started attacking with the broom."

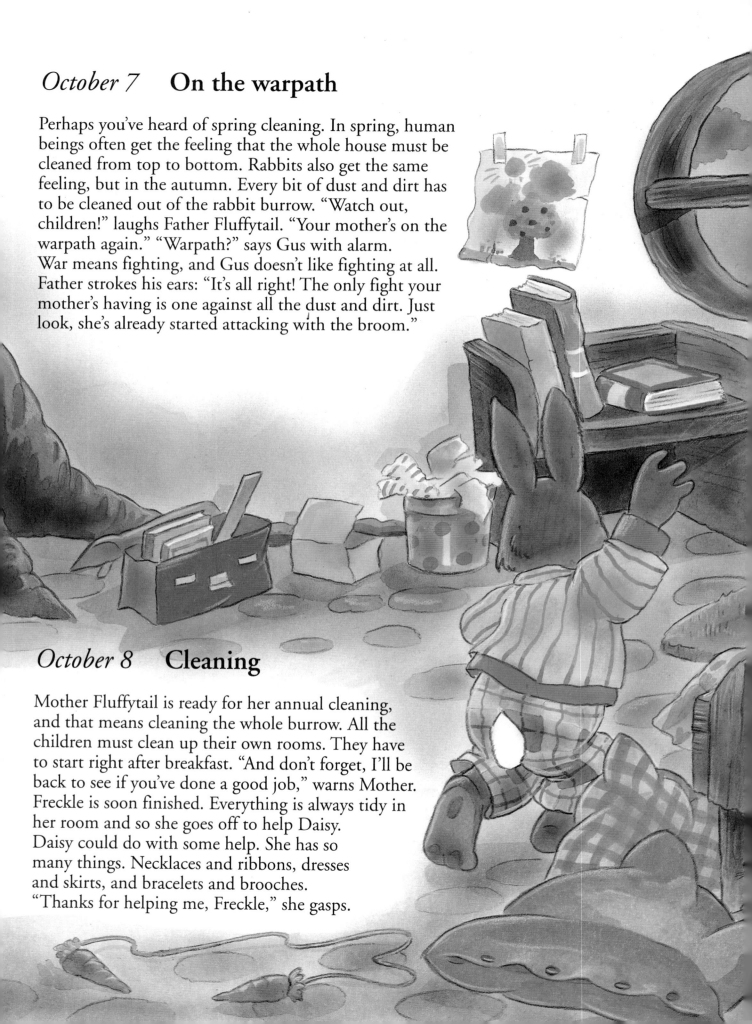

October 8   Cleaning

Mother Fluffytail is ready for her annual cleaning, and that means cleaning the whole burrow. All the children must clean up their own rooms. They have to start right after breakfast. "And don't forget, I'll be back to see if you've done a good job," warns Mother. Freckle is soon finished. Everything is always tidy in her room and so she goes off to help Daisy. Daisy could do with some help. She has so many things. Necklaces and ribbons, dresses and skirts, and bracelets and brooches. "Thanks for helping me, Freckle," she gasps.

October 9   Inspection

Mrs. Fluffytail is checking all the rooms. She's already seen Charlie, Gus, Billy and Harry. Now it's Hip and Hop's turn. What *is* going on? Instead of cleaning up, they're having a pillow fight. "Stop that!" says Mother. "Work first, then play!" Tom's room looks perfect. He's folded up his clothes and put them in tidy piles.

October 10

Empty

Mrs. Fluffytail has nearly finished her rounds. Roberta's room is the last one to be checked. Roberta has done her very best. The room looks very tidy. But her chest of drawers looks so empty! Mrs. Fluffytail can only see jeans and sweaters in it. Roberta has thrown away all her dresses! "I wasn't going to wear all those girlie things anyway!" says Roberta cheerfully.

October 11

Hairdresser

Daisy Fluffytail knows what she wants to be when she's grown up. She wants to be a hairdresser. She's already brushing and combing all day long as it is. She can't get enough of it. When she's finished with her own hair and tail, it's her brothers' and sisters' turn.
"Freckle, may I brush your hair?" she asks nicely. Freckle sighs. Well, all right. She does as Daisy asks and sits on a stool. A little later, Freckle has two little braids in her hair. Now it's someone else's turn.

October 12

Scissors

"Mother, may I borrow your scissors?" asks Daisy Fluffytail.
Mrs. Fluffytail is busy. Without thinking, she gives Daisy the kitchen scissors. Daisy cheerfully trots back to her room. Suddenly, Mrs. Fluffytail realizes that Daisy is playing her hairdresser game. And what do hairdressers do with scissors?
Mrs. Fluffytail runs as fast as she can to Daisy's room. My goodness! She's just in time. Daisy is about to start cutting Roberta's hair. "Stop!" shouts Mrs. Fluffytail. "You're not to do that!"
The two little rabbits look at her with long faces. Daisy looks sad because she's not allowed to cut Roberta's hair. Roberta looks sad because she was hoping so much to have a boy's haircut. Still, Mother has the last word.

October 13   **Highlights**

Daisy is looking for her brother Billy. She's already brushed and combed all her other brothers' and sisters' hair. Billy's the only one left to do. "No brush is going through my hair!" cries Billy as he shakes his tangled locks. But Daisy isn't so easily put off. "What about some highlights in your hair?" she asks. "A lot of rock stars have them." That sounds really good to Billy. If only he knew that Daisy has just picked some elderberries. She mashes up the berries and then dabs the juice onto his hair. Oh, what a shock when he looks in the mirror afterward! His hair has turned bright purple! He looks just dreadful! And mother is not only shocked, but also very cross. Daisy's not allowed to play at hairdressing ever again.

October 14

Why is it that they laugh?

Why is it that they laugh at me?
I think it's mean as mean can be.
Where'er I stand I hear them joke,
for it's at me that fun they poke.
They split their sides and point me out,
which leaves me with no shred of doubt.
Or else they stare with eyes so wide
at purple hair I cannot hide.
But *I* think it's just jealousy
and that they'd love to look like me.

October 15 **Fed up**

"I'm fed up with it!" moans Billy Fluffytail.
He's extremely cross with his sister, Daisy.
She said she would make him look like a rock
star. And look at him now! She's dyed his hair
bright purple. "Everyone's laughing at me,"
complains Billy. Mother Rabbit feels sorry for
her son. She fetches some soap from the
kitchen. "Come on, Billy, let's give that hair
of yours a good washing," she says.
But however much she washes and rinses, Billy's
hair stays bright purple. And all that washing only
makes it even bushier. It's standing up on end.
Billy will have to get a haircut.

190

October 16

Unusual

Look at that! You can't
help stare.
See his head of purple hair!
Who would want to
look so funny?
What a most
unusual bunny.
In the wood they think
it's silly.
All that hair belongs
to Billy.

October 17 **Mist**

Wispy tendrils of white mist
twist and thread like creeping vines
into branches, around the leaves,
on the ground and through the pines.
Could it be that this secret world
has been made a magic land,
wrapped in sheets of silver gauze,
by an elf or fairy's hand?

October 18

Ghost

Harry Fluffytail goes outside into the mist.
He can't stop thinking about Wild
Woodsman Dan. Long ago, Woodsman Dan
had chased away an evil ghost. The ghost was
white and could make itself as big as it
wanted. It was able to cover the whole Wild
Wood with its ghostly body. That was very bad
because the sun could no longer shine as long as
the ghost covered the wood. Trees and grass need
sunshine to grow and animals can't do
without it either. But what can
you do against a ghost?

October 19   **Blowing**

The animals thought for a long time. How could they chase away the white ghost that covered their wood? At long last, they came up with an answer. The ghost would have to be blown away. All the forest animals gathered together. They all stood in a row and began blowing. They blew as hard as they could. Puff! Puff! Their cheeks bulged and were fit to burst. "Ha! Ha!" laughed the ghost. "You'll never be rid of me that way." The animals were almost ready to give up. Whatever they did made no difference. Just then, a little rabbit came running up to join them. Would that be any help?

October 20   **An example**

"Ha! Ha!" laughed the white ghost. "Is that tiny little rabbit supposed to blow me away?" But the ghost didn't know that *this* little rabbit was very good at blowing. He also didn't know that his name was Dan. "Come on! Everyone together! One, two, three!" Well, thought the others, if the little rabbit wasn't giving up, then they wouldn't give up either. For the last time, they took a very deep breath and then...they blew so hard that the white ghost flew right out of the wood. "Hooray! Three cheers for Dan!" they shouted. "An example for all animals to come!" Dan became a famous hero, of course. And to this day, whenever a mist comes down, you'll still see rabbits blowing it away.

October 21 **Autumn**

Grandpa and Grandma have been staying with the Fluffytail family for three weeks. It's time for them to go back to their own burrow now. "Why do you have to go back so soon, Grandpa?" asks Hip. "Because autumn is coming," explains Grandpa. "And once autumn is in the air, the cold of winter will not be far behind." "But how do you know that it's autumn, Grandpa?" asks Hip. "Just look around," says Grandpa, pointing. "You can see all sorts of things that tell you it's autumn." Hip and Hop look all around. Will they be able to spot any autumn things? "This is just like 'I spy'!" laughs Hop. "Yes," agrees Grandpa. "Wait I'll give you a clue. It's red with little white spots."

Do you know what Grandpa means?

October 22   Toadstools

Toadstools, toadstools, everywhere. The whole wood is full of toadstools. Yesterday, when Grandma and Grandpa left, there were only a few of them. But now it looks like it's been raining toadstools in the night. They're all over the place and in all kinds of colors. "Do you think that pixies live in toadstools?" Hop asks Hip. "Only in toadstools that have a front door," replies Hip. Hop spends all day looking for a toadstool with a door, but she doesn't find one. What a pity.

October 23

Pixies

Hop goes to see Father Rabbit. "Father, do you know where pixies live?" Father lifts Hop onto his lap. "Not in toadstools. They live in little holes under the ground. A toadstool sometimes grows above their hole in the autumn. Then it looks like that's where they live." Hop understands now. "I was wondering where all the pixies lived in summer and winter, when there aren't any toadstools."

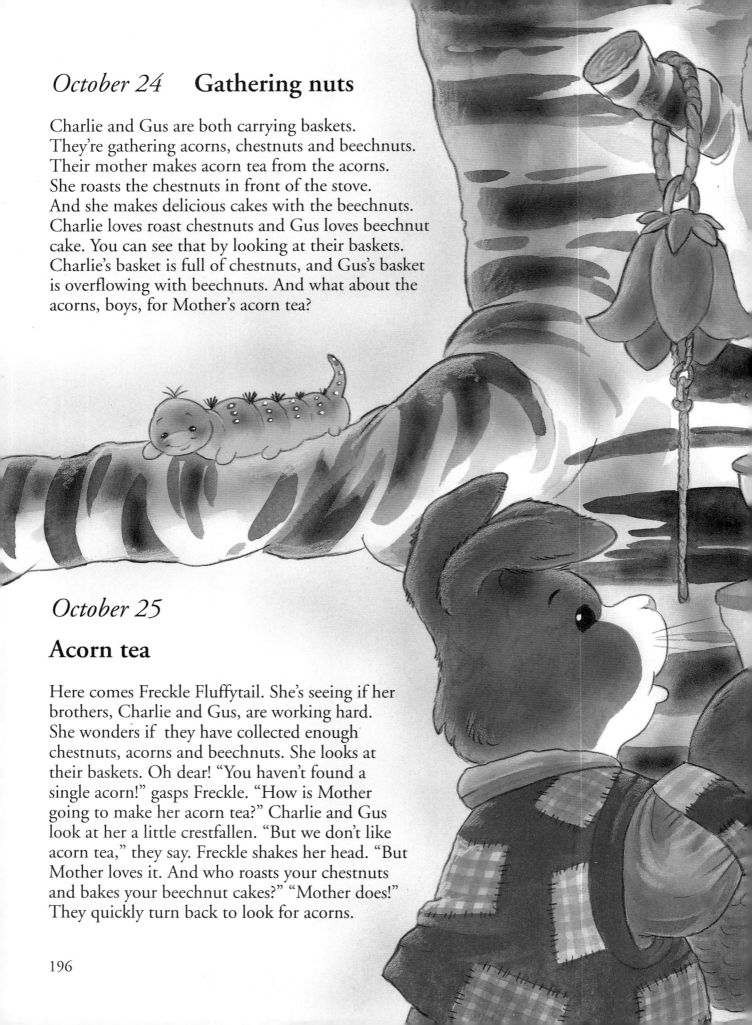

October 24   Gathering nuts

Charlie and Gus are both carrying baskets.
They're gathering acorns, chestnuts and beechnuts.
Their mother makes acorn tea from the acorns.
She roasts the chestnuts in front of the stove.
And she makes delicious cakes with the beechnuts.
Charlie loves roast chestnuts and Gus loves beechnut
cake. You can see that by looking at their baskets.
Charlie's basket is full of chestnuts, and Gus's basket
is overflowing with beechnuts. And what about the
acorns, boys, for Mother's acorn tea?

October 25

Acorn tea

Here comes Freckle Fluffytail. She's seeing if her
brothers, Charlie and Gus, are working hard.
She wonders if they have collected enough
chestnuts, acorns and beechnuts. She looks at
their baskets. Oh dear! "You haven't found a
single acorn!" gasps Freckle. "How is Mother
going to make her acorn tea?" Charlie and Gus
look at her a little crestfallen. "But we don't like
acorn tea," they say. Freckle shakes her head. "But
Mother loves it. And who roasts your chestnuts
and bakes your beechnut cakes?" "Mother does!"
They quickly turn back to look for acorns.

October 26 **Trading**

Freckle, Charlie, and Gus are trying to find acorns for their mother. But they can't find any. "Are you looking for something?" comes a little voice from a tree. It's Hazel the Squirrel. "We're looking for acorns for our mother's acorn tea," explain the three rabbits. Hazel has already collected a big store of acorns for the winter. He'd like to give the Fluffytails something, but he needs to have something to eat himself. "If I give you some of my acorns, what will I get back in return?" he asks. "All my chestnuts!" cries out Charlie right away. "And all my beechnuts!" calls out Gus cheerfully. The exchange is soon made. Good news for Mother!

October 27

Huntsmen

The shrill blast of horns sounds all through the Wild Wood. As soon as they hear the sound, all the animals dive into their holes. They know what it means: there are hunters in the woods. Father and Mother Fluffytail count their children. Are they all inside? One, two, three, four, five, six, seven, eight, nine, ten, eleven. Thank goodness! Then, Father makes sure that the front door is firmly locked. "It'll be a very clever bloodhound that's able to get in here now!" he says with a smile. Even so, the children don't feel completely safe. They listen to every sound with pricked-up ears. The hunting horn suddenly sounds very close by. They shut their eyes in fear.

October 28 **Poor Rusty**

Rusty the Fox has heard the hunters too. But he doesn't duck into his hole. He knows that the bloodhounds have very keen noses. They follow every trace and find every hole. They're especially good at following foxes. Rusty flees deep into the woods.
"Taratatataa!" goes the hunting horn. "Woof! Woof! Woof!" go the bloodhounds. Rusty is scared half to death. He runs and runs, but the hunters are getting ever closer. He runs until he comes to a hill. It's Rabbit Hill. From a window in their burrow, the little Fluffytails can see the poor fox running for his life. "He's just made it," says Harry, "but they'll get him soon!" But Freckle feels sorry for the fox. Can't they help him?

October 29   **Not fair!**

The Fluffytails want to help Rusty. They don't think it's fair. All those hunters going after one little fox. So, Mother Rabbit collects all the pepper shakers she can and hands them out. "Quick!" she says. "Put pepper on the fox's trail before the hunters get here!" Harry, Leaper, and Father Fluffytail are the fastest runners. They put pepper all over the fox's trail. Then, they go back inside. And here come the bloodhounds! "Woof! Atchoo! Woof! Atchoo!" go the dogs. Because of all the pepper, they can't smell anything any more. The hunters can't understand it, but as their dogs have lost the scent, they decide to go back home again. Rusty has been saved!

October 30 **Stringing apples**

Some food keeps for a very long time. Potatoes, for instance. But other things can rot or go bad. Fruit goes moldy if you keep it too long. But even apples can be kept for a long time if you only know how. You can cut an apple into slices and then dry them out. Freckle and Daisy Fluffytail are threading pieces of apple onto a string. Then, they hang up the apple strings in the loft for them to dry. "Don't they look pretty?" says Freckle. "Yes," agrees Daisy, "they look like party decorations. Just like for someone's birthday." It makes them feel like singing a song.

October 31

Apple-stringing song

When we're busy apple stringing
We can't help but start singing
Needle, thread, oh la-di-da,
Apples red, oh tra-la-la!

Give me one more apple ring.
Listen how it makes me sing.
The prettiest apple string by far
Oh fal-di-di and tra-la-la!

201

November 1　**Windy**

The Wild Wood looks beautiful in the fall. Some trees turn completely yellow, while others turn a fiery red. The wind adores the brightly colored leaves too. "Wooo! Whoosh!" it blows, and carries off the leaves, one by one. The wind takes them up into the air and then down they flutter to the ground. But the wind won't leave them be, even then. "Wooo! Whoosh!" blows the wind, and it piles a great heap of leaves up against the rabbit-hole door. "Oh my!" says Father Fluffytail. "Soon we won't be able to get outside. Come on, children! We have some sweeping to do."

November 2

What happened?

Father Fluffytail scratches his head. He just can't understand it. Only ten minutes ago he'd swept up the last of all the fallen leaves. But look at it now! He angrily waves his fist at the wind. But then he sees Leaper. Leaper's having the greatest fun! He jumps right into the middle of the tidy heap of leaves. When Leaper hops out again, his father's tidy heap is a big untidy mess all over again.

202

November 3   Migrating birds

How cold and dreary it is, but Tom and Gus still want to
play outdoors. They stamp on the ground with their rabbit
feet to keep warm. "I wish I was a migrating bird," says Tom.
Gus looks at him and frowns. "What's a migrating bird?" he asks.
Tom looks into the sky and sighs: "It's very cold for birds in
winter. So in fall, before it snows, a lot of birds fly off south
to warmer countries. It's called migrating." Gus thinks that it sounds
like a nice idea. "Are those countries far from here?" he asks.
"Much too far," sighs Tom.

November 4   Far

Some birds, as I am sure you know,
like neither snow nor ice,
and migrate in the winter to
a summer paradise.
So off they fly to distant lands.
A thousand miles they'll roam,
and wait until spring comes again
before they fly back home.

November 5 Sammy

Sammy the Swallow can't go on any longer. He has to take a rest. He's on his way to South America with his whole family. That's where they go every year to spend the winter. But South America is such a long way off. Sammy perches on a branch. "Are you a migrating bird?" he hears someone ask him. It's Gus Fluffytail. "Yes." Sammy nods. "I'm a swallow." "And are you on your way to a warm country?" asks Gus. "Yes." Sammy nods again.

November 6

A difficult journey

Sammy the Swallow is talking to Gus. "My journey is not only very long, but also dangerous. Sometimes a storm can blow up out of nowhere. And we sometimes meet with birds of prey too." "Why do you go then?" asks Gus. "For food," says Sammy. "Swallows eat flies. But there aren't enough flies here in winter. That's why we go to South America. There are always flies to eat there."

November 7 Difficult game

All the little rabbits love playing board games. When it's raining outside and the wind is blowing, they sit nice and snug in their burrow. Each one takes a turn in choosing a game to play. Today, it's Tom's turn to choose. He knows which game he'd like to choose right away. He'd like to play chess. But chess is only for two players and there are eleven of them. And chess is a very difficult game as well. Tom knows that none of his brothers and sisters will be interested. They'd rather play a game where you can laugh and have fun at the same time. "Let's play...Fox and Ladders," says Tom at last.

November 8 Playing

The Fluffytails are playing Fox and Ladders. They take turns throwing the dice and then counting the dots on them. Next, they move forward by the same number of squares. On some squares you find yourself at the bottom of a ladder. That's good because you can climb up it and get closer to the end of the game. But at the top of the ladders there is a fox. If you land on that, you're sent all the way back down the ladder and you start all over again! Leaper's having really bad luck today. "Stupid game!" he calls out crossly. The others laugh. "Come out from under the table, Leaper, or do you want a ladder?"

November 9   Cross

Are you feeling really cross?
Feeling blue and at a loss?
Make a smile. Go on, just do!
Soon you'll feel as good as new.

November 10

Little lights

Little sparkling lights at night.
Twinking jewels that shine so bright.
Lanterns keeping dark at bay,
turning nighttime into day.

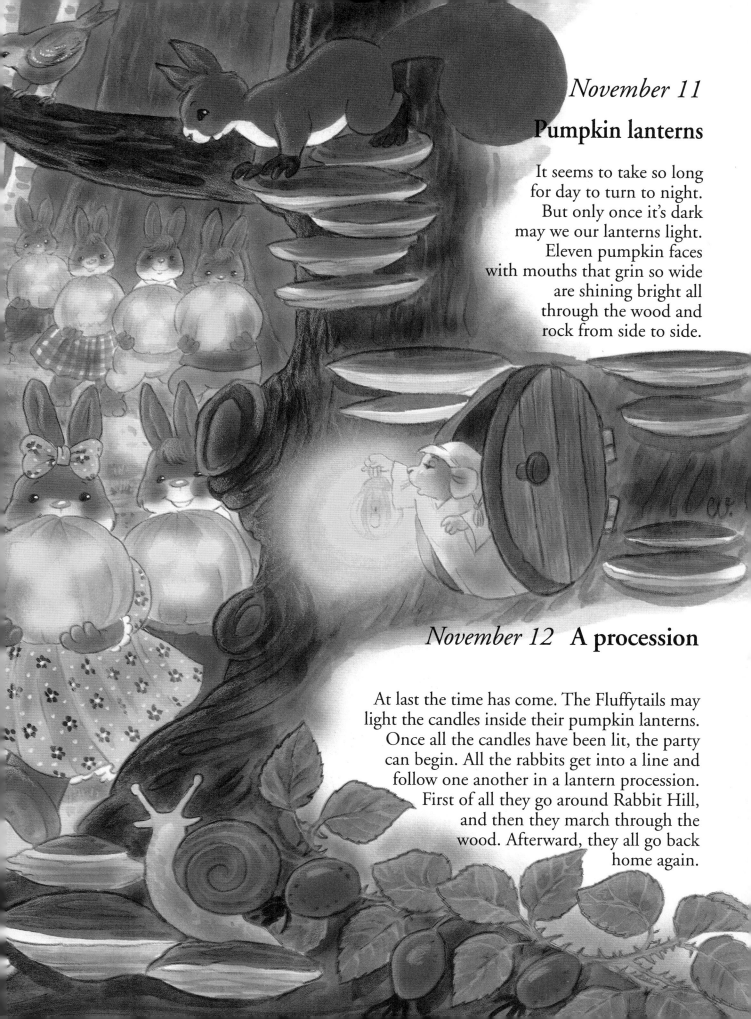

November 11

Pumpkin lanterns

It seems to take so long
for day to turn to night.
But only once it's dark
may we our lanterns light.
Eleven pumpkin faces
with mouths that grin so wide
are shining bright all
through the wood and
rock from side to side.

November 12 A procession

At last the time has come. The Fluffytails may
light the candles inside their pumpkin lanterns.
Once all the candles have been lit, the party
can begin. All the rabbits get into a line and
follow one another in a lantern procession.
First of all they go around Rabbit Hill,
and then they march through the
wood. Afterward, they all go back
home again.

November 13

Escape

Roberta Fluffytail slips quietly outside. Nobody must know. She's going to hide. Only when she's a safe distance from the rabbit burrow does she stop for breath. "So! I managed to escape that easily enough!" she laughs, pleased with herself. "Cheep! Cheep! What have you escaped?" asks Percy Sparrow. "Sybil the Spider!" gasps Roberta with relief. "Are you scared of spiders?" asks Percy with surprise. "Me? Scared? No way!" laughs Roberta. "But Sybil comes to give us knitting lessons. And if there's one thing that I think is a waste of time, it's knitting!"

November 14

How stupid!

Roberta Fluffytail managed to escape before Sybil the Spider arrived. Sybil gives the Fluffytail girls knitting lessons. "Knit one, pearl one, and pull through. How stupid!" sings Roberta. But who is it that she sees walking toward her on eight long legs? "Oh no!" gasps Roberta. "It's Sybil!" It's too late to hide. Sybil has seen her. "Roberta!" says Sybil. "How nice of you to meet me. Now we can walk to your burrow together." Roberta can't get out of her knitting lesson now. How stupid, she thinks.

November 15   Knitting lesson

There Roberta sits, along with Freckle, Daisy and Hop. They're being given a knitting lesson by Sybil the Spider. Each of them is holding a pair of long knitting needles. Sybil first teaches them how to do the beginning stitches. "Ten stitches are enough to start with," says the spider. "Put the needle through the first loop, pull the thread around it and pull it carefully through the loop." Biting her lip with concentration, Roberta tries. But whatever she does, the thread slips off her needle.

November 16   Tied up in knots

"Look how well it's going!" says Daisy cheerfully. She proudly shows them what she has knitted. "Very clever!" says Sybil the Spider. Then she looks at how the other Fluffytail sisters are getting on. Hop and Freckle have already come a long way with their knitting. But what about Roberta?
"Oh dear!" says Sybil. "What have you done, Roberta?" Her wool has wrapped itself all around her feet and ears. In fact, there is wool just everywhere except on her knitting needles. "I think my knitting's a bit knotted," mumbles the little rabbit to Sybil.

211

November 17   Itchy

Itch, scratch, itch.
Twist and twitch.
I'm scratching here.
I'm scratching there.
There's something prickling
in my hair.

November 18

Winter fur

"Don't scratch, children!" says Mrs. Fluffytail
sternly. It's always the same at this time of year.
Now that it's getting colder outside, the rabbits
are losing their light summer fur. A thicker coat
of winter fur is growing in its place. But it makes
them feel terribly itchy. Mrs. Fluffytail takes out
a great big comb. "Time for the November
combing," she says, clapping her hands.
One by one, her children are going to have
their fur coats thoroughly combed.

November 19 **Nasty comb**

"Ooh! That feels better," sighs Harry Fluffytail. Mother has just given him a good combing. She used her big comb to get rid of all that itchy old summer fur. All that nasty scratching has stopped at last. His brothers and sisters have been combed as well and feel much better for it. Billy is the only one still to be done, and he's hidden under the table. Billy hates having his fur combed so much that he'd rather be itching. But Mother doesn't agree. She bends under the table, takes Billy by the ear, and puts him on a stool. "Everyone is being combed, and that means you too!"

November 20 **Next year**

Billy Fluffytail is sitting on a stool, feeling miserable. The comb is pulling its way through his fur. But Billy's fur is so full of tufts and knots that the comb doesn't have an easy job. "Ow! Ouch!" Billy keeps crying out. At long last, his fur is completely combed. "Phew!" he grumbles. "I won't hide next year!" "Good, Billy," laughs his mother. "You see. It wasn't so bad after all." "Yes, it was!" cries Billy. "Next year, I'll hide the comb!"

November 21

Animals in winter

Father Fluffytail opens the *Great Guidebook for Rabbits*. Tonight, he's going to read to his children about animals in winter. But before he starts, he asks them: "Who can tell me what animals do when winter comes?" "I can!" says Tom, sticking up his arm. "Well, go on," says Father.
Tom is a bit of a know-it-all, and so he says: "Migrating birds fly off to warmer lands, and the squirrels bring in their winter store of nuts, and..." Charlie suddenly interrupts him. "And the cleverest animals sleep through the whole winter!"
Tom may know a lot, but when it comes to sleeping, Charlie is the expert.

November 22   Why?

Father Fluffytail nods and smiles. His children seem to know a lot. "Do you know *why* some birds fly away and *why* some animals sleep through the winter?" he asks. All is quiet. Even Tom doesn't answer. All at once, Gus speaks up: "So they won't be hungry!" "Very good, Gus!" Father pats Gus on the back. "How did you know that?" Gus tells him about his talk with Sammy the Swallow. Sammy told him that he flew to South America every winter because there were always flies for him to eat there. "Asking someone is cheating!" Tom cries out. Do you think Tom is perhaps a little jealous?

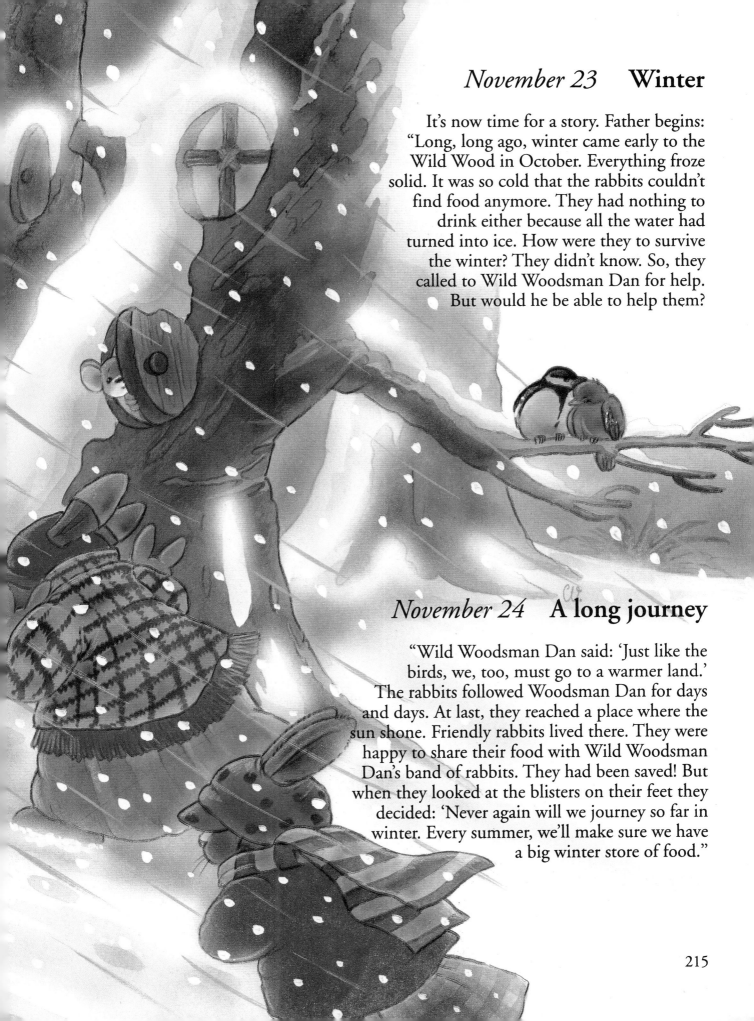

November 23   **Winter**

It's now time for a story. Father begins: "Long, long ago, winter came early to the Wild Wood in October. Everything froze solid. It was so cold that the rabbits couldn't find food anymore. They had nothing to drink either because all the water had turned into ice. How were they to survive the winter? They didn't know. So, they called to Wild Woodsman Dan for help. But would he be able to help them?

November 24   **A long journey**

"Wild Woodsman Dan said: 'Just like the birds, we, too, must go to a warmer land.' The rabbits followed Woodsman Dan for days and days. At last, they reached a place where the sun shone. Friendly rabbits lived there. They were happy to share their food with Wild Woodsman Dan's band of rabbits. They had been saved! But when they looked at the blisters on their feet they decided: 'Never again will we journey so far in winter. Every summer, we'll make sure we have a big winter store of food.'"

November 25   Sleepy

Harry Fluffytail thinks his brother, Charlie, is
boring. Charlie just spends all day sleeping.
"What a waste of time!" cries Harry. But Charlie doesn't
think that it's a waste of time at all. His bed is so nice and
soft! "I wish I was a bear," he sighs. "Then I'd be able to
sleep all winter long. That's what all bears do. Then Harry
would be a bear too, because he's my brother. He'd have
to sleep all winter as well!" Just imagine Harry sleeping
all winter! It's such a funny idea that Charlie can't help
giggling from underneath the covers.

November 26 **Cold as ice**

"I'm going to give that brother of mine a fright," mutters Harry to himself. He thinks it's really silly that Charlie spends all day asleep. If it goes on, he thinks, then Charlie will be asleep all winter. Perhaps bears can do that, but rabbits can't. They still have to eat from time to time. Harry has thought of a plan. "Charlie says how nice and warm his bed is," he chuckles. "In that case I'll need something cold. As cold as ice!" What is Harry up to?

November 27 **The last laugh**

Harry is a naughty rabbit. He wants to give his brother a fright. He takes some ice cubes out of the freezer and then goes off to find Charlie. He's asleep under the covers, of course. He slips the ice cubes between the sheets, one by one. The ice cubes start to melt at once. "Huh?" says Charlie, waking up. "It's all cold and wet!" Charlie is soaked to the skin. But Harry has made a mistake. "Oh no!" he gasps. "That's *my* bed! What are you doing in *my* bed, Charlie?" "Mother wanted to change the sheets on mine," replies Charlie. "So I crawled into yours instead." He who laughs last laughs longest.

November 28   **Woolly hats**

"Button your jackets if you're going outside, and pull your woolly hats down over your ears!" says Mrs. Fluffytail to Hip and Hop. The twins do as she asks. It's not easy pulling a woolly hat over such long ears but they manage it. Hip and Hop like wearing their woolly hats and they're such nice ones too. Mother knitted them herself. She made a bright blue one for Hip and a bright red one for Hop. Once she'd finished knitting, she used some white wool to put a little star on Hop's hat, and a little moon on Hip's hat. "Now everyone can tell which of you is Hip and which of you is Hop," she says. The twins look so alike that even their father makes a mistake sometimes.

November 29

Earache

My ears ache from the cold.
Inside my hat they're rolled.
But earflaps may, they say,
keep all that cold at bay.

Earflaps

"Hats tight on!" his mother told. "Outside it is very cold." Gus's hat of warmest wool was too small. If he didn't wear a hat, he'd be frozen quick as that. Mother had some good advice: "When you're once more on the ice, I'll make earflaps just for you, otherwise you'll turn bright blue."

December 1

Careful

My, my! It's so slippery! It looks as if the whole world has been turned into a skating rink. A thin layer of ice is lying everywhere on the ground. The Fluffytails have to be careful when they go outside. But if you're Leaper Fluffytail, you can't do anything carefully or slowly. As soon as he sets foot outside he land on his behind. He scrabbles back up again, takes a big jump and...whoops!...there he goes again! "Be a bit more careful!" Freckle warns her brother. "Your tail will soon be black and blue!"

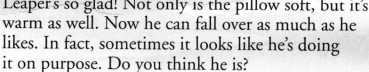

December 2

On purpose

Freckle Fluffytail feels sorry for Leaper. He loves leaping and jumping so much. But the ground is so icy that it's as slippery as soap. He must have landed on his behind a hundred times by now. His tail is freezing and it hurts.
Freckle fetches a pillow and a piece of rope from the attic. "I'm going to tie this pillow to your behind," she says to Leaper. "Then at least you'll have a soft landing if you slip over."
Leaper's so glad! Not only is the pillow soft, but it's warm as well. Now he can fall over as much as he likes. In fact, sometimes it looks like he's doing it on purpose. Do you think he is?

December 3

Yippee!

How thrilled the Fluffytails were
when through the glass they spied
a crispy carpet of white snow
piled thick on every side.
"It's snowball-throwing time!"
they shout.
But Mother soon complains:
"I don't mind that you're having fun,
but watch my windowpanes!"

December 4

Snow

It has snowed all night in the
Wild Wood. Rabbit Hill now
lies underneath a thick, white
blanket of snow. How excited the
little Fluffytails are when they see it.
They finish breakfast double-quick
because they want to be outside as
soon as possible.
"Let's have a snowball fight!"
shouts Harry. His nose is still
covered in porridge.
Mrs. Fluffytail shakes her head.
Shouldn't she tell him to wash his
face first? Oh, never mind. Just this
once she lets him play outside without
making a fuss. After all, it is the first
snow of the year.

December 5

Snowball fight

"Plop!" The first snowball lands on Gus's nose.
"Got you!" laughs Harry.
Harry runs straight outdoors once breakfast is over. There was no stopping him. While his brothers and sisters are still putting on their jackets and coats, he is busy making a big pile of snowballs. Every time one of them pokes a head out of the rabbit hole, Harry is able to hit them with a snowball. But the others don't leave it at that. "Just you wait, Harry. We'll get you!" they shout, and so a snowball fight breaks out.

December 6

Oh my! oh my!

The Fluffytails are having the greatest fun. They're having a snowball fight. "Whoosh!" go the snowballs, whizzing through the air. "Whoosh! Whoosh!" and then..."Crash! Tinkle!" Oh my! Oh my! One of the snowballs has broken a pane of glass! An angry Mrs. Fluffytail rushes outside. "Who did that?" she scolds. The children look at each other. They're not sure. They were having such fun that they didn't really notice. "We all did it," says Gus in the end. Mrs. Fluffytail understands and says: "You can all pay for a new windowpane and from now on, any snowball throwing is to be done a long way from our rabbit burrow."

223

December 7   Orange crate

A thick layer of snow is still lying all over the Wild Wood.
Hip and Hop have asked Father for an old orange crate.
They carry the crate to the top of Rabbit Hill. Once on
the top, Hip climbs into the crate and Hop gives him
a push. "Swoosh!" Hip slides off down the hill.
"It's absolutely the greatest feeling!" he says. It's Hop's
turn next. "Push me!" she says to Hip.
But Hip pushes her so hard that Hop and the crate
turn upside down. Hop doesn't think
there's anything so great about that!

December 8   Drawing

"You should all have a nice sleigh," says Father
Fluffytail. "I know what, let's make one ourselves."
What a good idea! The little Fluffytails want to
start right away. They go in search of two strong
planks of wood. Tom gets some paper and a pencil
at the same time. He's going to make a drawing.
He's going to draw his idea of how the sleigh
should look. Tom can draw so well! He starts
off with some neat, straight lines, and very
soon he has made a beautiful drawing
of a sleigh. Tom has even put in the
measurements. Now they
can really get to work!

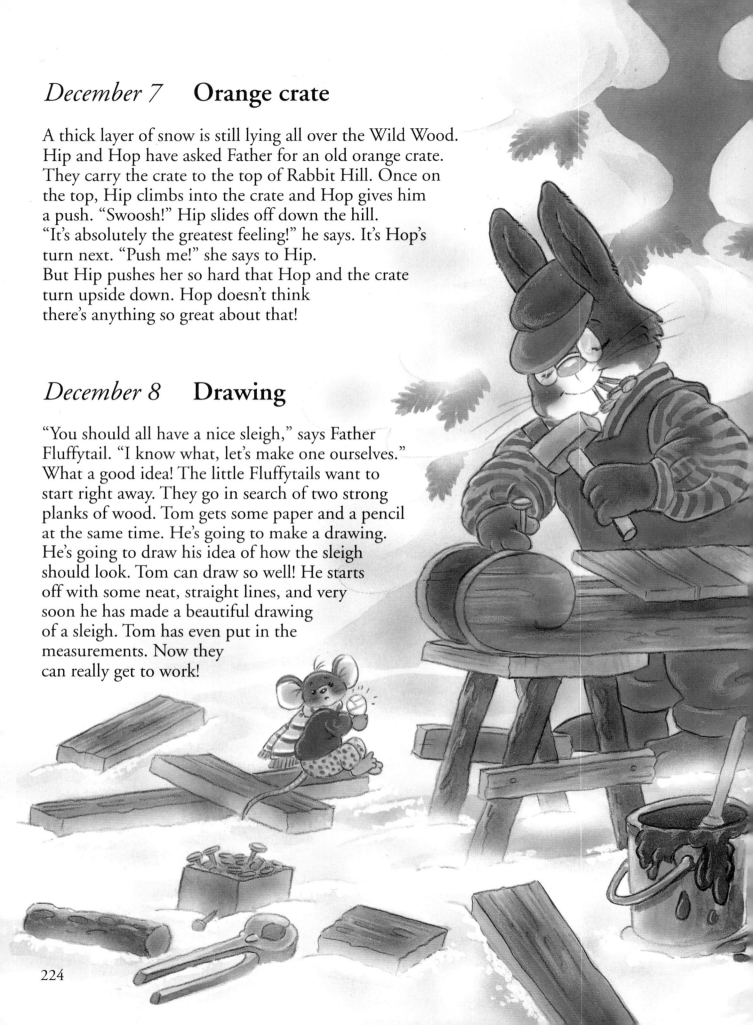

224

December 9   Sawing

The little Fluffytails are helping to saw and build
a sleigh with their father. "It's going to be the best
sleigh in the whole world!" says Billy. Father even lets
him hammer in a nail. He swings back the hammer and...it
hits Leaper right on the nose!
"Ouch!" cries Leaper. "That hurts!" Billy's so shocked
that he forgets to look at what he's doing. "Bang! Ouch!"
Now he's hit himself on the paw. Father wraps a bandage
around it and puts a Band-Aid on Leaper's nose.
He hammers in the rest of the nails himself.

December 10   Sliding

My sleigh and I
can nearly fly.
We slide so fast,
we zoom straight past.

225

December 11 **Robin**

Harry Fluffytail is in seventh heaven.
He loves snow and ice. He sat in the sleigh
for hours this morning. Now he's taking great
hops through the snow. "Oh, how lovely the
snow is; if only it could always be winter,"
he sings. High in his tree, Robin Redbreast
is watching him. "If you say so!" he pipes up.
"I can't get into my nest." Harry laughs.
"Did you lock the door and lose your key?"
"Oh, you can joke all you like,"
twitters the bird crossly, "but just
wait until icicles start hanging
down to block your
front door."

December 12 **Icicles**

The poor little robin can't
get into his nest anymore.
Icicles are hanging down in
front of his door. They're too
big for him to break with
his small beak. "Wait,"
says Harry. "I'll get rid of
the icicles for you." "Can
you really do that?" chirps
Robin. "They're very thick
and hard." "But I'm very
strong," boasts Harry. "I'm nearly as strong
as Wild Woodsman Dan." "We'll see," sighs
Robin, who doesn't really believe him. He
shows Harry where the nest is.

December 13 **Popsicle**

Harry Fluffytail pulls on an icicle as hard as he can. "Oooph!" It's so cold and hard! But Harry doesn't give up. If the icicles stay there, Robin Redbreast won't be able to get to his warm nest again. "Oooph!" Harry's little feet start to hurt from the cold. And the icicle is still there, as solid as ever. It starts to make Harry angry. "Stupid Popsicle!" he says. Hey, that's a thought. Suddenly, Harry stops feeling so angry. He has an idea. "Wait here!" he says to the robin. "I'm going to get my brothers and sisters." What can Harry be planning?

December 14 **Get licking!**

Robin Redbreast is waiting impatiently for Harry Fluffytail. Harry promised that he would get rid of the icicles in front of Robin's nest. However, to do that he needs help from his brothers and sisters. Do you think it's because they're stronger than he is? Oh, look! Here they come, all eleven of them. "What do we have to do, Harry?" asks Gus Fluffytail. Harry points and says: "Those icicles in front of Robin's nest have to go. They're too big to break off. But I suddenly thought how much they looked like Popsicles. If we all start licking them, the icicles will be gone in no time." "What are we waiting for?" says Gus. "Let's get licking!"

December 15   **A strange noise**

Mrs. Fluffytail is in the kitchen. She put a lot more logs in the stove than normal this morning. It's cold outside and so she's going to make a thick pea soup for all the family. "That'll warm them up," she thinks.
She fetches the peas from the pantry. She's just about to put the soup pan on the stove when she hears a noise. "Snrrk! Snrrk!" it goes.
"What a strange noise," says Mrs. Fluffytail. "It seems to be coming from the stove. She listens again and, yes, it is coming from the stove.
"Snrrk! Snrrk!" goes the stove.

December 16

Broken

"Come quickly!" Mrs. Fluffytail calls to her husband. "I'm afraid that the stove is broken. It's making such a strange noise."
Mr. Fluffytail appears at once. The stove broken? In the middle of winter? That's not good at all. He gives the chimney a tap and takes a peek at the fire. But the noise carries on.
"Snrrrk! Snrrrk! Snrrrk!"
Father Fluffytail scratches behind his ear. He's never seen anything like this before. He can't understand it. All at once, he notices a strange smell as well. It smells a little like burning fur!

December 17   Coughing?

A stove making a strange noise and also making a strange smell! It can't be a good sign. Mr. Fluffytail fills a bucket with water. The stove must be put out before it explodes! He empties the whole bucket over the stove all at once. The stove starts hissing and coughing. Coughing? A stove can't cough, can it? Then, two long ears suddenly appear from behind the stove. Charlie's ears! And they look a little singed. Father and Mother Fluffytail now see what has happened. That sleepyhead, Charlie, had fallen asleep behind the stove. The strange noise was from his snoring, and the strange smell was from the fur on his ears burning. Oh, Charlie! Really!

December 18

Hiccups

My, oh my, it must be
sick.
A stove that hiccups, hic, hic!
What is all the
noise about?
Quickly put the
fire out!
Father really cannot
find
the origins of
the smell.
But it seems to be
burning rabbit fur.

December 19   A package

"Oh my goodness!" grumbles Dickie the Carrier Pigeon. He mops
at his brow. He's never had to deliver a package quite as big as this
before. The package he's delivering to the Fluffytail family is so
big that he has to ask seven other carrier pigeons to help him.
And even with eight of them, they can only just move it.
"I wonder what's inside?" he groans. There are stamps
on it from a faraway country. "We won't go until
the Fluffytails have opened the package.
I want to see what's inside after
making all this effort."

December 20   Too lazy

Just look. The carrier pigeons have brought the
Fluffytail family a big package. They're all
waiting in a row to see what's inside.
The Fluffytail children are very
curious too. They can hardly
wait for Father to open it.
"Open With Care" is printed
on the package. Father cuts
carefully through the string
with a knife. But just as he's
about to open the package, it
suddenly starts to wobble and
shake.
It shakes itself open. And what
steps out? Uncle Simon. What a
surprise! Dickie the carrier pigeon
nearly falls flat on his back.
"Now I've seen everything!"
he says. "Were you too lazy to
use your own two feet?"

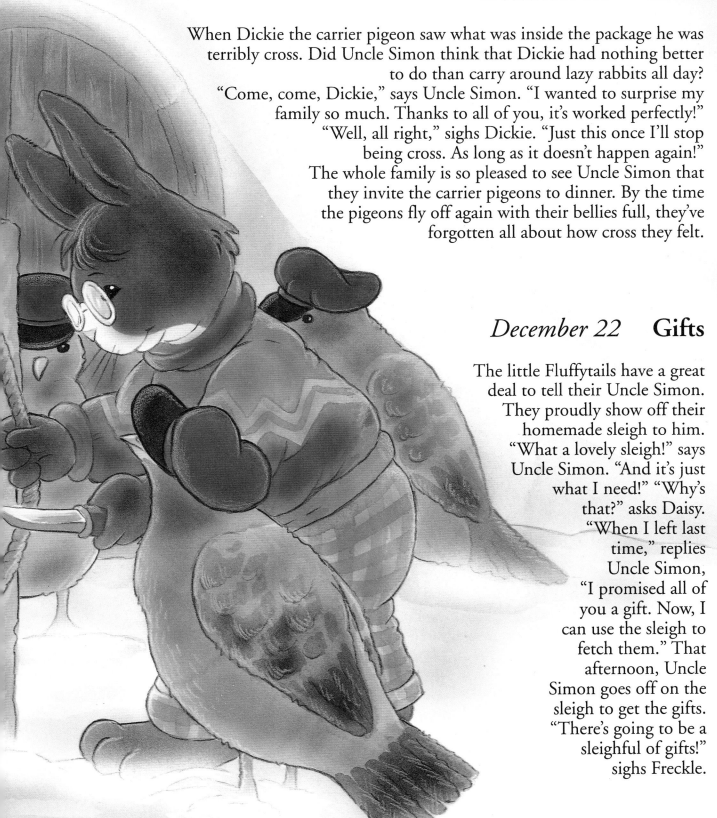

December 21 **Cross**

When Dickie the carrier pigeon saw what was inside the package he was terribly cross. Did Uncle Simon think that Dickie had nothing better to do than carry around lazy rabbits all day?
"Come, come, Dickie," says Uncle Simon. "I wanted to surprise my family so much. Thanks to all of you, it's worked perfectly!"
"Well, all right," sighs Dickie. "Just this once I'll stop being cross. As long as it doesn't happen again!"
The whole family is so pleased to see Uncle Simon that they invite the carrier pigeons to dinner. By the time the pigeons fly off again with their bellies full, they've forgotten all about how cross they felt.

December 22 **Gifts**

The little Fluffytails have a great deal to tell their Uncle Simon. They proudly show off their homemade sleigh to him. "What a lovely sleigh!" says Uncle Simon. "And it's just what I need!" "Why's that?" asks Daisy. "When I left last time," replies Uncle Simon, "I promised all of you a gift. Now, I can use the sleigh to fetch them." That afternoon, Uncle Simon goes off on the sleigh to get the gifts. "There's going to be a sleighful of gifts!" sighs Freckle.

December 23 Christmas Story

Daisy Fluffytail listens to her father with great,
wide eyes. He's reading the little rabbits
a Christmas story about animals who were always
arguing and fighting with each other.
Until Christmas, that is. Beneath the
pine trees they decided to live in peace.
"We'll never fight again. We won't hate
each other anymore," they said. "From
now on, we'll live together happily in
peace." Daisy sighs when the story is over.
What a beautiful story it was. She
promises herself never to fight
again and to be kind
to everyone.

December 24

Friendship

Tonight it's Christmas Eve. Daisy Fluffytail is
thinking hard. "Before Christmas Day comes, I want to
be friends with everyone," she decides. "Friends with
everyone in the whole Wild Wood." So she puts on her coat.
She's going to make friends with Rusty the Fox. When Rusty sees
Daisy coming, his mouth starts to water. "Well, I'll be bunny-
hopped!" he slurps. "What a delicious Christmas dinner that tender
little rabbit will make." But all the same, he's still very curious to
know what Daisy wants. Daisy wants to tell him the Christmas
story. She talks and talks. The story is so long that it makes the fox
sleepy. He yawns, his eyes start to get heavy, and...he begins to
snore. He *is* tired, thinks Daisy, and we *still* haven't made friends.

December 25 **Peace on earth**

Do you know the reason
for the Christmas season?
Men wish earthly peace to all,
to animals both great and small.
All our fighting quickly ends.
At Christmastime we all make friends.
A joyous time of fun and mirth.
A festival of peace on earth.

December 26 **Christmas decorations**

Perhaps you have a Christmas tree in your house
at Christmas. Perhaps it's covered in decorations
and lights, maybe even real candles.
But a Christmas tree is much too big if you
live in a rabbit burrow. That's why the Fluffytails
have decorated their burrow inside and out with
pine tree branches. They've fixed branches around
the windows and they've made a wreath from
them that hangs on the front door.
Mother has placed a row of candles in the
window as well. She lights them once it's
dark and then the burrow looks just as festive
from outside as it does indoors.
Freckle thinks it's so pretty that
she often pops out just to look.
Only for a little while; otherwise she
gets too cold.

December 27   Naughty angel

It's cozy and warm in the Fluffytail family's living room...and very quiet. Uncle Simon is sitting in front of the stove in Father's big armchair. He's taking a nap. The children are not allowed to make a noise and only whisper. Suddenly, Harry starts to giggle. A pine tree branch is hanging just above uncle's nose. A little angel is dangling from the end of the branch. Whenever Uncle breathes out, the angel wobbles. Harry gently bends the branch down so that the angel's little wings tickle his uncle's nose. "Ah...ah... tchooo!" Uncle wakes up. Harry says quickly: "The little angel did it. It must've wanted you to tell a story." Clever Harry!

December 28   Christmas at sea

Uncle Simon stares at the candles in the window. Their little flames remind him of something that happened long ago, and he starts to tell a story: "It was Christmas. I was on board my ship and the sea was cold and gray. Everyone's teeth were chattering. The compass had frozen solid, and we were lost. We were too scared to remember about Christmas. We had given up hope, when just then we saw fire on the horizon. The captain set course for the fire and after a while we arrived in Fireland. The Firelanders were celebrating Christmas by lighting great bonfires on the beach. That's how we were saved. All because it was Christmas."

December 29   Forbidden

"For the last time, no!" says Father Fluffytail strictly. "You may not set off any fireworks. It's much too dangerous!" Gus, Charlie and Harry look at each other with disappointment. It's such a shame. They'd been so looking forward to it. "Not even one little firecracker?" asks Charlie again.
"No, not even one," replies their father. "On New Year's Eve, we're all going to sit together by the fire. I want all my children in one piece. As a member of the rabbit fire brigade, I've seen a lot of accidents with fireworks." Gus, Charlie and Harry know that he is right, but it's still a shame.

December 30

Bang!

The Fluffytail family is sitting next to the fire. Father has read them stories and they've played some games. "All those games have made me hungry," says Mother. She goes to the kitchen and soon comes back with a basket full of nuts. There are all kinds: hazelnuts, walnuts, and chestnuts. "Delicious! Roasted chestnuts!" says Father, and he puts a few in the fire at once. Then, they carry on with their game. Suddenly there's an enormous bang, and lots of little pops. The fire's heat has made all the chestnuts burst open. Harry jumps for joy. "Gosh, Father! You said we wouldn't have any firecrackers this year!"

December 31   **New Year's Eve**

A New Year's Eve party,
and it's already late.
Eleven small rabbits
are allowed to stay up and wait.
They're waiting till midnight,
and then it's all fun!
For when the clock strikes,
they can kiss everyone.
And then, all in chorus,
the rabbits will cheer,
and wish every one of us
a happy new year!